STRANDED

STRANDED

MELINDA BRAUN

Simon Pulse
New York   London   Toronto   Sydney   New Delhi

SIMON PULSE
An imprint of Simon & Schuster Children's Publishing Division
1230 Avenue of the Americas, New York, New York 10020
First Simon Pulse hardcover edition August 2015
Text copyright © 2015 by Simon & Schuster, Inc.
Jacket photo-illustration copyright © 2015 by Steve Gardner/Pixelworks Studios
All rights reserved, including the right of reproduction in whole or in part in any form.
SIMON PULSE and colophon are registered trademarks of Simon & Schuster, Inc.
For information about special discounts for bulk purchases,
please contact Simon & Schuster Special Sales at 1-866-506-1949
or business@simonandschuster.com.
The Simon & Schuster Speakers Bureau can bring authors to your live event.
For more information or to book an event contact
the Simon & Schuster Speakers Bureau at 1-866-248-3049
or visit our website at www.simonspeakers.com.
Jacket designed by Jessica Handelman
Interior designed by Mike Rosamilia
The text of this book was set in Goudy Old Style.
Manufactured in the United States of America
2 4 6 8 10 9 7 5 3 1
This book has been cataloged with the Library of Congress.
ISBN 978-1-4814-3819-3 (hc)
ISBN 978-1-4814-3821-6 (eBook)

To my father-in-law, John Joseph Braun, who always greets
me by asking, "So how's the writing coming?"
Here you go.

And to my parents, James and Susan Dahlstrom, for the
countless bedtime stories.

One Year Ago

I inhaled and choked. No air. Just cold, dirty water, thick with grit, rushing into my mouth.

Instantly my throat contracted, squeezing shut as my lungs refused the liquid. Gagging, I spit back.

Help me!

Panic shot my hands out, snapping my eyes open. Green fog stared back, everything a watery blur. My arms jerked spastically; my legs followed.

No! I heaved forward, but the strap across my chest wrenched me back. My fingers fluttered automatically, an instinctual muscle memory, until they found the release button.

My chest burned, despite the cold, and my hands scrambled for the door latch. Unlocked. I slammed my shoulder against it, but the weight of water slowed it to a weak shove. It didn't budge. I shoved again, and my elbow jabbed out the open window. Rolled down—I remembered it now. But only when I somersaulted out of my seat and my head hit the roof, did I understand I was upside down. I twisted and rolled, my entire brain consumed with finding an exit. *Air. I need air. Just one gulp.* Spots flickered and faded in front of my face like fireflies. *How long has it been? Thirty seconds? Get out! Get out now!*

As I pushed myself through the window, something hot stabbed into the underside of my arm. Glass, metal, I couldn't tell, only that it bit into my skin like teeth, the sting clearing my brain for a second. *Up! Go up!* I flipped over again and pulled my head around, forcing myself to keep my eyes open. Light above me. A round golden blob, flickering down on me through the water, shiny as a brass ball. The sun. The surface. My fingers clawed through weeds and grit and muck like an animal escaping a trap.

I pushed off as the last stream of bubbles flew from my mouth, pulling hard strokes, hand over hand, shedding my flip-flops with each kick, and in four strokes I broke the surface. The blue-and-gold light blinded my burning eyes, and my mouth flew open to scream. But the only sound I heard was the howling gasp of relief I made as air rushed in.

Immediately a voice cut through my panting heaves. "I got you! I got you!" Strong hands pulled my shoulders back.

"No!" I lurched away, spluttering. "Stop!"

"It's okay! You're gonna be okay."

"No! More!"

"You're in shock!" The hands clamped down tighter, swirling the water around me into a dark whirlpool; I was too shaky to fight.

"More people!" I screeched, bending my head down in a weak attempt to bite his hand.

"In the car?" The grip relaxed slightly. "I didn't see anyone!"

"Backseat!" I kicked out, elbowing his chest, using his torso as a wall to shove off. "One more person!"

Down I dove, my eyes strained open in the murk. Everything was shadows, dark gray-and-green blobs. Then below, a darker hulk, but I only realized it was the car when my fist punched the tire. *Where is she?* My ears popped when I swallowed, my fingers ran over the underside of the fender. *Is this the back? Where is the back?*

I pushed through an open window and banged my face against the headrest, my hands finding nothing. Empty. But when I grabbed again, thin feathery wisps brushed against my arms. Tendrils like seaweed. Hair. *She's here.* My head throbbed dully as my fingers worked up the length of the seat belt—the click of the button like a gunshot in my ears. I pulled her from the belt, but her arms were already cold and soft, pieces of soggy dough that might come apart in my hands. I jerked her forward, hard as I could, screaming into the water.

A silver ceiling. Hanging tubes and cords and rows of knobs and buttons. Blinking red and yellow lights. I swung my head

3

around; my eyes rolled the opposite direction, spinning like forgotten marbles. Above my face, in front of white lights, someone said something to another person, a command or question, words that sounded like *Over here. Look at me. You're going to be all right. What is the ETA?* Were they talking to me? I couldn't answer. I didn't even care. I blinked and faded back to darkness.

A low buzz woke me. A hum—a repetitive mechanical beep keeping time with my heart. A cold hand gripped mine, then squeezed tightly as I blinked my eyes open. My mother's powdery perfume, dusty with the scent of lilies and roses, floated over me, and I lifted my head to ask the only thing I still didn't know. The plastic oxygen mask muffled my voice, but my mother knew what I asked. It was only a word. One question.

Under the fluorescent lights her eyes shimmered like rain-soaked pavement, but she didn't speak. She didn't say a word. She only bent her head forward and turned it, hiding her face away from mine.

Then I knew the answer.

Day 1
Late Morning

"Are you sure, Em? You don't have to go if you don't think you're ready."

"Christine, we've already discussed this. . . ."

"It's fine, Mom. We're already here," I said from the back-seat, watching the campers unload their gear in the gravel parking lot. They all seemed healthy. Strong and tan. Farm kids? City kids? The kind of kids whose moms probably had milk and cookies waiting for them after their varsity tennis meets or swim club. I focused on the back of one boy, lanky, shaggy hair, wearing a bright turquoise T-shirt and lugging a well-stuffed backpack over one shoulder. It was one of those serious models with a lightweight aluminum cage, water-proof ripstop nylon, and a million different hidey-holes. I had the same one.

I pressed my head against the window. "Besides, you've already paid for it."

"Honey, that's not important. If you don't feel up to it . . ."

"I know, Mom. But Dr. Nguyen thinks it will be a good thing. So do I," I tacked on at the end. *What I feel is irrelevant. It doesn't matter. It doesn't change anything.*

"Okay. Well, I'm just saying . . ." My mom stopped. Her voice was thin, stretched tight like a layer of ice over water. It wouldn't take much to break it. But I couldn't stand to see her start crying. Not again. Not here. You'd think a person would get to a point where they had nothing left. Like a well of water. Eventually you have to run dry, don't you?

"It's only a week," I reminded her. "And when I get back, I'll look into some of those college applications, okay?" There. That should convince her. It convinced my dad. I watched his shoulders sink behind the backrest, as if he was an inflatable device someone just stuck with a pin.

"That's good to hear, Emma," he said. "You could sign up for a few community college courses. Transfer in next semester."

I put my hand on the door latch. "That's the plan," I lied, knowing the deadline had already passed for the local community college fall semester. Over the past year my lies were coming faster and easier, sliding out of my mouth like spit. "It's cheaper to take the prereqs there, anyway." My dad smiled and nodded at the rearview mirror as he opened his door, satisfied.

I got out too; I didn't want my mom to see my face. My dad was easy to convince. He *wanted* to be convinced. He didn't look too far below the surface of things—I used to think it was because he didn't believe anything was there, but now I know better. Some people just don't want to turn over the rock and see the worms.

I stepped into the hot sun and stretched my arms over my head. Despite the heat, there was a smell in the air that reminded me of the inside of a freezer. The north woods had its own scent, and after a five-hour drive north we'd gone just about as far as you can go without crossing the Canadian border. Ely, Minnesota, to be exact. Population 3,471. Give or take. The gateway to the Boundary Waters Canoe Area, or BWCA, as the locals say. Last dot on the map before the wilderness.

My dad handed me my backpack with a smile. I don't know why he bought something like this; I never camp. Correction: We (the Dodd family) never camp. Have never camped. The closest we got was when I was ten and we stayed in a cabin at Jellystone Park.

But this whole thing had been my idea. I saw the BWCA brochure while I was waiting my turn in the counselor's office. I suppose I could have done homework, but that would have been a responsible use of my time. Instead I went through the stack of pamphlets on the table next to my chair, or, as I called them, illustrated cautionary tales. STDs. Smoking. Drugs. Drunk driving. The entire "don't do it or you'll be sorry" catalog, fanned out for my perusal.

I shuffled them like a deck of playing cards, until a flyer on the wall caught my eye. It was bright yellow, with a large outline of a bird on the top. A loon, I think. I could barely read the words, so I got up and walked over and ignored the sideways glance the receptionist gave me.

DO YOU HAVE WHAT IT TAKES?
Probably not.

HAVE YOU ALWAYS WANTED TO TEST YOUR LIMITS IN THE GREAT OUTDOORS?
Not especially.

LEARN TO LIVE OFF THE LAND BY YOUR WITS?
Shit, no. Most of those pioneers died of dysentery. I like my indoor plumbing, thanks.

BE A LEADER IN LIFE?
Uh, I'm a pretty good follower.

THEN JOIN US FOR A WEEK THAT WILL CHANGE YOUR LIFE!
Really? Only a week?

I stopped reading right there and ripped the flyer off the wall. I suppose I just could have written the information down and looked it up later, but some part of me knew that if I left the office without it, it would just be one more thing I failed to follow through on. I needed to steal it. Thankfully, the receptionist was too busy on the phone to notice.

That night I typed the website address into the computer.

It looked to be a non-Jesusy vacation adventure in the Boundary Waters. Very Boy Scouty. Very Outward Bound-ish. It was for teenagers at least fifteen. I stared at the pictures of perfect forest landscapes, fiery pink-and-orange sunsets, an owl perched up in a pine tree, people paddling canoes over lakes that looked like mirrors. There, I thought. I needed to go there. I hovered the cursor over the reservation tab, already knowing the conversation I would have with my parents. What I would say. What they would say. How I already knew this was a good idea. It was a forgone conclusion, as they say. A done deal. I clicked the button.

But that had been back in the beginning of April, when there were still dirty scabs of snow on the ground. Summer seemed impossible. Now it was the second week of August, and I stood blinking stupidly in the sun, wondering where I had put my sunglasses, while my dad unloaded all the gear from the back, smiling like it was Everest base camp and he was my own personal porter.

"Got everything?" My mom climbed out of the passenger seat.

"Yep." I didn't have a lot. Tents were provided, as were our meals. According to the website, campers were responsible for bringing a sleeping bag, hiking boots, a canteen, flashlight, warm jacket, gloves, sweatshirt, sweats, quick-dry hiking pants, personal toiletries, socks, sandals, swimsuit, sunblock, a hat, and of course (and probably most importantly) bug spray.

"Enough Off?"

"Two cans," I said. "With extra deet." I slung my new backpack over my shoulders and buckled the straps across my waist and chest. Despite being stuffed to the gills, the thing didn't feel very heavy. "I've got everything I need."

"Almost." My dad pressed something cold and smooth into my palm. "Take this."

I opened my hand to see a faded red Swiss Army knife. A *knife?* I swallowed and looked at my feet.

"David." My mom's voice wavered.

"I don't need this," I blurted. "Really, it's okay. It's not like we're going to have to hunt a moose or something."

My dad laughed. "You'd need more than that for a moose." My dad had hunted growing up. Hunted, fished, camped. But he was the only one in our family who enjoyed such things. My mom had always been more of a four-star-hotel type of person. Eggs benedict and bacon (extra crispy) for breakfast.

"And," my dad continued, "You probably won't need it. But you never know. . . ." He trailed off, looking over my head and refusing to acknowledge my mom's ashen face. The past year had been bad between them—I was the only one in the family seeing a shrink, but I certainly wasn't the only one who needed it. *I wonder if they'll get divorced.* In some ways it already seemed inevitable.

Yes, they definitely needed professional help. *Professional help*. I personally preferred the term "headshrinker." I always imagined some voodoo priest in face paint, his shaman stick dangling with a bunch of tiny shrunken heads.

I wonder what Dr. Nguyen would say if I told her that. Maybe want to give me medication. Then again, maybe not. I wasn't crazy, technically. And I wasn't suicidal, not really. I had bad thoughts. Dark thoughts. Horrible nightmares. Dr. Nguyen called it PTSD—post-traumatic stress disorder. Her words, not mine. Apparently I now had a disorder I thought was reserved only for soldiers who'd been in combat.

So the fact that my father was giving me a weapon and sending me off into the wilderness with total strangers made me think two things simultaneously:

My dad really trusts me.

My dad is crazier than I am.

"Thanks, Dad." I didn't open the blades but tucked it quickly into the back pocket of my jeans. "I know it was Grandpa's. I'll make sure to take good care of it."

"From the war." My dad nodded. "He said it was lucky. He said it saved his life."

"Okay." I didn't know what else to say to that.

My parents hugged me hard, too tight and too long, but I let them, barely flinching when my mom kissed my cheek.

"I love you, Emma."

"Me too." It was all I could manage. I couldn't bring myself to say the words even if I felt them. "See you next week." I shrugged out of their arms and turned toward the far side of the lot, to where a pack of kids had gathered in front of an older man with a salt-and-pepper beard, faded Twins ball cap, and mirrored aviator shades. He stood under a hand-painted sign (INTO THE WOODS) and held a clipboard. There was a shiny silver whistle around his neck, so I guessed he was in charge. That's all you needed to look official. Sunglasses, clipboard, whistle. He could be a serial killer for all we knew.

I crunched across the hot gravel in my new hiking boots, following a tall, athletic-looking girl with a red bandana tied around her forehead. *She's probably done this before.*

I was in decent shape, physically speaking, but I had never portaged a canoe. This girl had strong-looking shoulders, with well-defined arm muscles—she could probably portage canoes in her sleep.

"Welcome, everyone!" The bearded man waved us closer. "This is going to be some trip! The day's a-wasting, so hustle up!"

Hustle up? He sounded like my JV basketball coach.

"My name's Chris, and I'll be your team leader and guide. Are you guys ready for the week of your life?"

Crickets. I looked around. Four boys, two girls, including myself. *This is it?*

"Um," said the tall girl, saying what everyone else was probably thinking. "Where's everyone else?"

"We can take up to nine," Chris explained. "But there were a couple cancellations."

"Great," said the girl, almost to herself. She turned around and winked at me, probably as relieved as I was that there was at least one other female. "Looks like a total sausage fest," she whispered, but loud enough for everyone to hear.

I liked her immediately.

Chris scanned the sheet on the board. "Are you Emma or Chloe?"

"Chloe Johnson," replied the girl smoothly, not missing a beat. She stepped back so we were standing next to each other. "This here is my sister, Emma."

Chris looked up, then down, then back up at me. "Emma Dodd?"

"That's me," I said, instantly hating how unconfident I sounded, as if I was apologizing for being there.

"All right," said Chris. "Where is Isaac Bergstrom?"

"Here." A tall blond boy sitting on the picnic table answered.

"Jeremy Vernon?"

"Yep."

"Wes Villarreal?"

"Here."

Wes and Jeremy stood side by side, obviously friends. They had probably decided to sign up together, which was a smart idea. Once again it hadn't occurred to me to ask one of my friends, though my friends had been in short supply the past year. Only Shelly still called me to hang out, though I usually never did. Most everyone else avoided me, socially speaking. Can't say that I blamed them.

"Oscar O'Brien?"

"That's me." It was the boy in the turquoise T-shirt. He pushed his glasses back up the bridge of his nose.

"Great, looks like we're all here. Let's go." Chris turned and started walking, and we all stood there momentarily, as if the whole idea was just a joke. Isaac slid off the table and followed; the rest of us did the same.

"We're going to the outfitters," Chris explained as he walked us to a large white conversion van. *Serial-killer van.* "We'll pick up our food and supplies, sign in, and go through a safety check." He opened a van door and motioned us forward. "Time's a-wasting! We got a lot of ground to cover in a week. Literally."

The sun disappeared behind a thick cloud, and an icy breeze gusted down over the treetops, making me shiver through my sweat. A warning? I think in the movies they called that foreshadowing.

This is probably a bad idea. I couldn't help the thought; it made me turn around and look for my parent's dark gray Subaru. But they had already gone.

"I think I'm going through withdrawal," Chloe said. "I practically got the shakes."

"Phone?" I spread the nylon tent out on the smoothest layer of dirt and leaves I could find, checking for stones and pinecones, then glanced over only to see that Isaac and Oscar had theirs up already. Wes and Jeremy were also done, now busy helping Chris gather rocks for the campfire.

Chris had let us send a farewell text to our contacts to let them know we'd all be incommunicado for the week. I sent one to my mom. *No phones 4 the week. C u soon. Luv Em.*

I figured she'd tell my dad. He wasn't much of a phone person anyway.

Then we turned them off and put them in a blaze-orange waterproof zip sack, and that was that. It didn't bother me too much. Nobody called me anymore anyway, and I dropped mine into the bag with a shrug. "Don't feel like you're missing anything, kiddos." Chris smiled as if he knew exactly what we were missing. "You'll survive without them for a few days."

"Yep, total phone withdrawal. I miss my music." Chloe snapped the telescoping rods into place, eyeballing the length of the two longest. "Does it matter which goes where? They both look the same."

"Uh?" I shrugged. "I don't know." Chris had said that our first challenge was to put our tents up. No directions. Which would be easy enough if either of us had ever put up a tent before. "If they're the same it shouldn't matter." I spread out a pile of six L-shaped metal stakes. "These must go in the straps." I tugged on the black loops at the base of the tent. "Let's do this part first."

After twenty more minutes we had it done, more or less. The entrance was facing the opposite direction from the others, but neither of us cared. After we put in our sleeping bags and packs, I crawled out to see all four boys watching us, curious grins on their mouths. Chris sat across the site, marking something on his clipboard with a pen. Maybe he was grading us. Either an A for effort or an F-minus for speed.

"You girls sure are slow," Isaac said.

I blushed and pressed a rock into the dirt with my heel. We *were* slow.

"What's your point?" Chloe asked.

Isaac crossed his arms and bobbed his head, smiling like a slimy used-car salesman, as if his point were glaringly obvious.

"Have you guys ever put up a tent before?" Wes grinned, but it wasn't the taunting one Isaac had plastered across his face.

"Heck, no," said Chloe. "And no directions, either."

Wes ran his hand through a thick shock of sandy-brown hair. "Well, then, you actually put it up pretty fast," he laughed. He wasn't very good-looking, not like the other guys, but he had an agreeable bulldoggish manner that made me like him instantly.

Isaac stopped grinning.

"Thanks!" Chloe flashed him a brilliant smile, transforming her face into something even more gorgeous than normal.

"No problem." Now it was Wes's turn to blush.

"Okay, campers," Chris called out, waving the clipboard

at us like a flag. "Time to go over a few small reminders."

"Again?" Jeremy muttered. "I thought we went over all that at the outfitters."

Back in Ely, we had stopped at the Big Loon Outfitting Company to load up our week's worth of supplies, which were, in no particular order:

> 3 ultralight aluminum canoes
> 1 Kevlar kayak (for Chris)
> 7 life jackets and paddles
> Camp stove and fuel canister
> Eating utensils and a cookpot
> Soap
> Hand sanitizer
> Toilet paper
> Trash bags
> Matches
> Paper towels

Plus the huge cooler stuffed with three meals per person per day, including snacks. All packed according to park regulations, including everything from cereal and pancakes to pudding cups, hot dogs, marshmallows, and chicken enchiladas.

A massive map of the BWCA covered a wall inside the store. It was huge. Overwhelming, really. Hundreds of lakes dotted the green field in a constellation of blue blobs, an entire galaxy of trees and water in a universe of wilderness. *How can this be?* I knew there were still remote places like this, but it somehow seemed pretend, a fantasy you saw on television. Something that existed a hundred years ago, now replaced by an endless sea of strip malls and Walmarts.

But it was still here.

Standing there in the store with my expensive new backpack and hiking boots, the actual reality finally set in. This was the real outdoors. The end of civilization.

The wild.

Several route numbers decorated the map, arching up across the wide expanse of green, some extending all the way to the Quetico area of Canada. Chris said we would be signed in for Route #5—Fishing, Falls and Indian Tales. Whatever that meant. I found the spot on the map and read the little blurb underneath.

Days needed: 5+, Difficulty: Challenging. This route includes many lakes and several long portages.

Great.

"All right, let's gather around the fire," said Chris, snapping me back to reality. "Dinner's almost ready. I hope everyone likes burgers."

We all did. He could have said we were having fried cat with a side of squirrel, and I would have devoured it. I was hungry. Real hunger, not just ready to eat because it was a certain time of day, but hard-core, razor-blade-sharp-stomach-pains hungry. And we hadn't even gone that far today.

Chris passed around the plates and utensils. No glass or aluminum cans allowed. Every piece of trash we had to carry out.

Chris slapped the meat patties onto the cookstove; the smell brought tears to my eyes.

"Who wants it Sconnie style?" Chris held up a packet of cheese slices.

Our hands shot up. "Good choice." Chris laughed.

After a few minutes he flipped each burger and added a slice of cheese; we clutched our plates and drooled. "Y'all remind me of my dogs when it's feeding time." He grinned. "But that's to be expected. We didn't go far today—a few miles, but there were a few tough portages. And y'all did good your first day out. Real good." Chris pointed his spatula at each of us in turn. "But you're gonna be sore tomorrow, so I want each of you to drink at least one liter of water tonight. If anyone needs ibuprofen and doesn't have their own, I have some. The important thing to remember is that we take our time. I don't want anyone getting hurt." He looked back down at the cookstove. "Time to eat."

Don't want anyone getting hurt. I bit into my burger. Melted cheese seared the roof of my mouth, but I didn't care. Nobody ever wanted to get hurt. But it still happened, didn't it? No matter how careful you were, no matter how smart your plans. It happened anyway. It happened all the time.

Day 2
Morning

The mosquito buzzed by my ear, circling my head like an insect spacecraft. So much for bug spray. I was sweating like it was an Olympic sport. Beads of sweat ran down from my hairline, pooling under my chin, and dripped off like a leaking faucet with every step. I wanted to wipe it away. I wanted to swat that mosquito. Instead, I adjusted my grip on the aluminum canoe and took a slow breath. It seemed like we'd been doing this all morning. Walking with a canoe loaded with all our stuff. Like it was some sort of sick joke. Canoes were meant for water, right? Shouldn't we be paddling across some clear ice-blue lake? Admiring the scenery? Looking for fish?

"Good God," Chloe grunted from the front. "How much longer?"

We were the last ones in the caravan, trailing a good twenty yards back from Wes and Jeremy. Jeremy's orange shirt vanished and reappeared between the trees like a warning light. *It would be easy to get lost out here.* But the trail was wide and fairly obvious, and we'd seen other people this morning (mostly families). I couldn't imagine the Dodd family going on a trip like this, no matter how much my dad would have enjoyed it. Maybe my mom would agree if we stayed in one of those fancy resort lodges that dotted the shore of Lake Superior. I shook my head, partly to deflect the mosquito. Maybe she would have agreed to that a few years ago, but not anymore.

Chris lead the way, carrying his kayak by himself, so I guess we shouldn't be complaining. He told us last night around the campfire that people would get scarce by the morning of the third day, after we passed the waterfall and got into a really remote area.

I gripped my fingers along the canoe hull and breathed into the burn. If this wasn't remote already, I had no idea what the word meant.

"Stop." Chloe jerked to a halt, and I almost dropped my end.

"What's wrong?"

"Log."

"Another one?" I set the canoe down and shook out my arms, rolled my neck back and forth. I had a stash of ibuprofen and had taken three last night, then fallen into a dreamless sleep, a type of sleep I hadn't had in a long time, which was definitely better than the dreams I normally had. Technically I would call them nightmares.

"Okay," I said, getting a new hold on the canoe. "You go first, and then we'll slide it over."

Chloe picked up the front and slid it on top of the moss. This log was the biggest one yet, almost waist high, with the diameter of one of those giant semitrailer tires. I wondered how such a big tree could just fall down like that.

Chloe rolled to the other side, and I pushed the canoe to her before climbing over myself.

"That's number six," Chloe said.

"You'd think they'd have someone out here to clean up the trail."

"Guess this ain't Disneyland."

I laughed. "You got that right."

My shoulders ached. I wanted to sit down, just for a minute. Instead, I looked ahead for Jeremy's orange shirt. I couldn't see it. I couldn't even hear the others, not above the sound of my own labored breathing and grunting. A bubble of panic popped in my chest. *Where did they go?*

"Hey," said Chloe. "I think I finally see some water."

"Thank God."

The trail twisted right, and we followed a winding switchback. The path narrowed so tightly our bodies brushed the papery leaves growing beside it. *Better not be poison ivy. Or poison oak. Or poison something.* Through the trees, flashes of silver and blue, then a flash of orange.

Around the last switchback the trail opened up onto a slim pebbled beach. Gusts of air hit my face, like I had just walked past an air conditioner set on high. The lake was huge, over a mile across. Sunlight bounced off the surface, making me squint to see the far side, which ended in a dark line of trees.

"Welcome to Loon Lake." Chris smiled when we appeared on the beach. "We'll be heading north along the shore for two miles, going through a little inlet that will take us over to the waterfall." He pointed his finger up the shore. "You can't see it from here, but there is a nice beach and a place to swim. The water is cold out here but not too bad for swimming. We'll do lunch when we get there." Chris refolded his map and tucked it into his pocket. "Make sure to reapply your sunscreen before we get out on the water. You can get a burn in twenty minutes, and I don't want anyone keeling over with sunstroke. Wear your hat."

The lake was a relief from the wooded trail, chilled with the smell of green plants and rusted iron. On the shore I exchanged my boots for Tevas, then waded in and dunked my head completely, cramming my wet ponytail into the baseball cap I'd borrowed from my dad, a faded baby-blue Brewers cap.

"Nice hat," Isaac said.

"Thanks," I replied, soaking my bandana.

"It wasn't a compliment."

I looked at him, his forehead wrinkled with horizontal lines, mouth screwed up in a pucker like he'd smelled something bad.

What's his problem? "You don't like baseball or something?"

I draped the bandana over my shoulder, debating dunking my entire body, clothes and all, but I was only wearing a light T-shirt. I didn't feel like nipping out in front of a bunch of guys.

"Or something," he said, sounding annoyed. He adjusted his own ball cap, curving the brim into a tight U with his hands, which appeared to be about twice the size of my own.

He's not much for words, this guy. He's probably a Twins fan.

"Whatever," I muttered, and helped Chloe put our backpacks in the canoe. When I coated my arms with sunblock, I saw Oscar watching me (or was he looking at Chloe?). I held out the bottle. "Need some?"

"I'm okay, thanks." Oscar smiled and dropped his gaze, suddenly busy with his life jacket.

"Yeah," Isaac interrupted. He winked suggestively while twirling his paddle like a baton. "I think he does need some."

I wasn't talking to you. I capped the sunblock shut, ignoring him, and shoved it back into my pack.

"What? Aren't you gonna ask if I need some?"

"Nope." I glanced back, glad to be wearing sunglasses, as if that could hide the expression on my face. "I think you're good." He had that milky pale skin that looked like it would burn in five minutes, and he also looked like the type of guy who'd rather fry than put on sunblock.

"That's right!" Isaac laughed, before hardening his expression to a leer. "I am." His voice was a low moan, and he gave me an obvious wink. "I definitely am."

I think I'm gonna be sick.

Despite the sun, a shiver raced up my spine, and I climbed into the canoe, scooting hurriedly to the front, careful to keep my paddle balanced on my lap as the waves hit the hull with hollow metallic slaps. And with one quick shove from Chloe we were off the rocks, gliding out onto open water. I couldn't help but sigh with relief.

Chloe heard me and agreed. "Now this is more like it."

I turned around, grateful to be sitting. However long we had to paddle, I knew it would be a huge improvement over portaging. Chloe had her red bandana wrapped around her head, sunglasses on, and a paddle resting on her knees. "I looked online for days at all the pictures, but it doesn't compare to actually being here."

"I know." I had to admit it was a pretty good view. I dipped my paddle in, taking a tentative stroke. "I've never been this far up north."

"Like a whole other country."

What skills Chloe and I lacked during the portaging portion of the trip we made up for on the water. It was a natural thing for us in the canoe. We seemed to know when to switch our paddles and when I should let her steer, and our matched strokes glided us like an arrow over the surface. This was the part that didn't feel like work.

"What's that thing?" Chloe pointed over my shoulder, and I adjusted my sunglasses, squinting.

"A duck?"

"Nah," she said. "I saw it dive and come back up way over there. Do you think it's a loon?"

"Well, we are on Loon Lake." I scanned the flat water. The breeze was calm, the entire surface a perfect mirror of the sky.

The loon rose suddenly, like a miniature submarine breaching the surface, all bright black and glittering white, and so close I could count the speckles on its wings. It had a small silver fish pinched between its pointed beak; its blood-red eye blinked at us with reptilian detachment. I had never seen a bird this close; if I leaned over, I could touch it with my paddle.

The loon swallowed the fish in a slick gulp, and in another blink it was gone beneath our boat, black and white flashes reminding me of a swimming penguin.

I dipped my paddle back in and twirled it like a swizzle stick, my throat itching like I'd just swallowed a spoonful of sand. Something important had happened, but neither Chloe nor I spoke.

We paddled on. Chloe set the pace, maintaining a good distance between the kayak and the canoes, and we went along like that for a long while, enjoying the silence.

When the sun was overhead, we reached the inlet. I jumped out into waist-deep water, shocking myself to breathlessness, but after the long sweaty morning, I couldn't say that the sensation was unpleasant.

"Oooh!" A plunk and screech behind me let me know

that Chloe had just done the same. "That woke me up!"

"No kidding!" I exhaled, letting the cold bite into my legs, and we hauled the canoe up onto the sandy beach. I plopped down next to it, breathing as though I had just finished a race.

"A good swim will help," Chris said as he watched the rest of the caravan angling toward the beach. Isaac's canoe, I noticed with glee, was last, and a good distance off.

"Great idea," Chloe replied. "My arms feel like they're gonna fall off."

"You'll feel a lot better after a dip." Chris smiled. "Like brand new." He turned back as Wes and Jeremy glided in, grinning good-naturedly.

"We kept trying to catch up." Jeremy laughed. "You girls should try out for the Olympics."

"Is canoeing even an Olympic sport?" Chloe asked, appreciating the compliment.

"Oh, it is, and I'm sure you'd make the team," Wes said. "You sure you never did this before?"

"Pretty sure," Chloe replied. "I must have a good partner." She poked me in the arm, and I knew then if I'd met her as a kid, we would have been friends. Maybe we still could be.

"All right, who wants to go fishing with me?" Chris asked.

"Not me," Wes said. "I'm going swimming."

"Maybe Isaac will," Jeremy offered, trying to be polite, but the look on Chris's face made me believe I wasn't the only one who didn't like him. Strangely, this revelation didn't make me feel better.

"Maybe," Chris said, and nodded. He looked like he was two seconds from deciding to go by himself, but then Oscar and Isaac paddled in. From Oscar's expression I couldn't tell if he was exhausted or pissed off. Maybe both. He pulled the canoe up on the sand in silence, grabbed his gear, and trudged up the beach to the campsite, only flicking his eyes at me once, sort of a look of shared commiseration.

"Okay, campers," Chris said. "Take a swim, cool off, settle down, and I'll be back in a bit with some fish." He pointed (more like jabbed) a finger at Isaac. "How about you come with me. I don't like fishing alone." The way Chris said it made it an order, not a question, and he put the tackle box and rods into the canoe before Isaac even had a chance to protest.

"Whew," I heard Wes mutter to Jeremy after Chris and Isaac had paddled back out. "Dodged a bullet."

They don't like him either.

"C'mon." Chloe pulled me up the beach in the direction Oscar had gone. "Let's go swimming."

The waterfall beat down on my shoulders like a vigorous masseuse, working out the knots and stiffness in a few minutes. I gave my scalp a much-needed shampoo-free scrub, enjoying the feel of icy water coursing over my head.

"Aren't you gonna rinse off?" I really wanted to wash my hair, but Chris said the BWCA had a rule against bathing within 150 feet of water.

"No. I'm good. I . . . "

"Cannonball contest!" Wes shouted, interrupting Chloe. "Points for biggest splash! Bonus for creativity!" He jumped off the tallest boulder, tucked himself into a ball, and hit the water with a hollow plunk.

"Emma?" Jeremy waved at me. "You in?"

I shook my head and dismissed them with a wave and a smile. "No thanks!" A year ago I would have joined them, but now I waded onto the beach and sat down next to Chloe, who had climbed onto her beach towel and sprawled out to soak up the afternoon sunlight.

"Boys." Chloe raised her hand to shield her eyes. "They don't change, do they?"

"Some don't."

Jeremy jumped off the boulder and opened up into something that looked like a belly flop. He hit the water with a painful crack, and Wes responded by laughing like an idiot.

"You got a boyfriend?"

"No. You?"

Chloe sighed. "Not anymore." She sat up suddenly and examined the tangerine polish on her toenails. "It's probably for the best, though. Starting college in the fall. They say you should be single."

"I've heard that." I suddenly did not want to have this conversation. I've never had a boyfriend, and I wasn't going to college in the fall. I wasn't going anywhere. I wanted to stand under the waterfall. I wanted to submerge myself and scream. I wanted to jump off those rocks like Jeremy and Wes and see how hard I could hit the surface. I wanted to break something so I could hear it shatter.

But I sat there, examining my own pink toenails and feeling as though I already had the beginnings of a sunburn. My skin itched and felt a size too small for my body.

"That one's been watching you," Chloe said quietly, and I glanced up. Wes and Jeremy were now busy trying to dunk each other—the sight made me ill. "Huh?"

"Not those morons." Chloe tilted her head to the side. "The one reading over there. The quiet one."

A worn-out paperback hid most of Oscar's face. He had dived into his book right after a quick swim, but he'd barely said a thing to either of us. Paddling canoes with Isaac hadn't put him in the best mood.

"You think?" I had caught him watching me when I was rinsing off in the waterfall. Definitely looking, but I couldn't tell what he'd decided.

"I know. Been staring at you like a puppy." She wiggled her toes in the sand, satisfied. "And I *know* that look."

"Maybe he was staring at *you*."

"Nuh-uh," she said. "You should go for it. He's pretty." She watched Oscar with a sideways glance. "Cute in a nerdy way."

"Yeah," I said. "Too pretty for me. I like to be the hot one in the relationship."

"I know what you mean." Chloe laughed, then sighed in resignation. "But I still like the pretty ones best."

We both laughed, loud enough for Oscar to look up from his book, and for a few seconds our eyes honed in on each other. Feeling nervous, I glanced at the cover in his hands, unable to read the title. *I should just get up and go ask him what he's reading. No harm in that.*

"Ugh!" Chloe screamed. "What the—"

I looked down. A humongous frog sat in Chloe's lap, blinking at us with a stunned expression. One more blink and then it jumped, leaping sideways at me, and I grabbed at it, cupping my hands to trap it against my thigh. The frog was slick and cold against my skin; the underside of its throat throbbed frantically against my fingertips.

Chloe jumped up like a cat whose tail had been stepped on, spinning around in midair. She glared at Wes, who grinned back as though he had just won the lottery. "What the hell is wrong with you?" she screeched.

"Dunno." Wes shrugged. *How does a teenage boy answer that question? How does anyone?*

I got up with the frog cupped carefully in my hands and waded back across the sandy shallows to the reeds. Oscar got up from his beach towel and followed me.

"What is it?" he asked. He stood close, just a foot or two away, and for the first time I could tell he was only an inch or so taller than me, but his chest and shoulders were tightly muscled, tanned the color of dark honey.

"Just a frog." His nearness flustered me, and I took a steadying breath. He smelled like wet rocks and sand.

"Can I see?"

I opened my hands immediately, smiling at the sound of his voice. Smooth and clean as the rest of him. The frog looked up, blinking deeply as it swallowed.

"Big one."

"Yeah." I couldn't think of anything else to say, too busy thinking of Chloe's observation. *That one's been watching you.* I glanced up. Red and gold strands in his dark brown hair glinted in the sunlight. Brown eyes, the same color as chocolate syrup, stared back at me. Oscar pushed his glasses back up his nose and smiled. At the frog. Not at me.

Trying not to let him see my blush, I turned back to the weeds. "I guess I should let him go over here."

"Hey there, campers!"

Isaac. He and Chris paddled to a slow stop behind us in their canoe.

"We've got dinner!" Chris lifted up a Styrofoam cooler with a promising smile on his face. He climbed out of the boat. "I bet you guys have never tasted fish this fresh!" Humming, he carried the cooler back up to the campsite.

Once Chris was out of earshot, Isaac stomped toward me. "Whaddya got there?"

"Nothing. It's just a frog."

"Let me see."

"Why do you—" The frog jumped out of my hands, landing on the sand in front of Isaac's feet.

"Ah, a nice fat one!" Isaac scooped him up immediately.

"Don't," I blurted. *Don't hurt it.*

"Don't?" Isaac's stare crawled up and down my body. He kept the frog cupped tightly in his hands, his eyes sharp as blue sparks.

"Did you catch anything?" Oscar asked.

"Did *I* catch anything?" Isaac repeated. "I don't know—is water wet?"

Oscar crossed his arms and blinked back at him with a hardness I hadn't seen before. A vein in his throat pulsed.

Isaac sighed, backpedaling only slightly. "I hope you like trout."

"I've never had trout."

"If you don't like it, you can cook this fatty up. He'd make a nice appetizer." Isaac gave the frog an air kiss. "Mmm. Yum yum."

"No thanks," Oscar said.

"Suit yourself." Isaac grinned and hurled the frog, throwing it like a major-league ballplayer. It flew over my head like a missile, whistling past the weeds until it hit the water with a dead crack. Isaac laughed and took his tackle box out of the canoe.

"What did you do that for?" Oscar asked, disgusted. He dropped his arms, his fists clenched at his sides.

I turned my head away, the space behind my eyes pricking

with heat, and took a slow careful breath. *Don't. Just don't let him see. Think of something else.*

"Huh?" Isaac gaped at Oscar as though he had just asked the question in Chinese.

"You *know* what."

"Relax, Wiener." Isaac shrugged, unconcerned. He'd already nicknamed Oscar "Wiener." Like the Oscar Mayer hot dog. *Good God, no wonder nobody can stand him.*

Isaac gave me another slick grin. "Like she said, it's just a frog." He turned around and strolled up the beach, whistling the entire way.

The loon called, the throaty vibrato sending a burst of nerves down my spine. I twirled my stick lightly, hovering my marshmallow carefully over the flames, my thoughts echoing like the mournful cry that drifted over the water.

Tomorrow. Tomorrow. August fifteenth. August fifteenth. Tomorrow is August fifteenth. It was one of the reasons (the main one) I chose this week for the trip, the reason I was here today on a lake with strangers and not back home in Hudson with my parents, wondering what to do with this day, wondering how I was going to get through it.

What would they do tomorrow night? Would my mom cook a special meal, or would she throw a frozen pizza in the oven? What was she doing right now? Pouring a double of vodka into a juice glass? I had seen her do that more often in the past year. Three glasses of wine with dinner. Sometimes the bottle instead of dinner.

I had no idea. And I didn't want to. How do you spend that kind of day? What are you supposed to do? Draw the shades? Light a candle? Say a prayer? What, exactly, is the protocol for the one-year anniversary of the death of your youngest child?

"Supposedly it's going to be a scorcher tomorrow," Chloe said suddenly, breaking the quiet. "At least, that's what Chris said." She pulled her stick from the flames, her marshmallow baked to a perfect doeskin tan. She slid it off and smushed it between two graham crackers. "Not a cloud in the sky. Perfect."

"Sounds like it." I nodded, wondering if she was referring to the weather or her marshmallow. I pulled my stick out of the fire, my marshmallow burning like a torch. I stabbed it back underneath a log. Another goner. But I wasn't hungry anyway, not after the trout and chicken enchilada dinner.

"All right, listen up," said Chris. He walked into the campfire circle with his all-weather radio in his hands. "Just heard a storm system is stewing in Canada. Possible snow coming in."

"Snow?" Wes snorted in disbelief. "In August?"

"It can happen," Chris replied. "And it could happen in a week."

"I thought we're supposed to be at the trail end by then," Oscar said. He had burned his marshmallows coal black and ate them right off the stick, no graham cracker required.

"Exactly," said Chris. "Which is why I want to get a move

on tomorrow, cover a few extra miles. Sounds like a whole mess of stuff is brewing up north, and I want to make sure we're in before it gets bad."

"Aye-aye, captain," said Isaac, and saluted, sounding moderately sarcastic. Chris gazed back, his face a blank mask in the firelight, until Isaac had the decency to look away.

"Do you think we'll really have a snowstorm?" Jeremy asked.

"Don't know." Chris's eyes left Isaac's face. "Maybe. Maybe not. Might just turn to sleet and rain. Maybe some thunderstorms along with it. The whole system could fall apart or miss us entirely." He tucked his radio back under one arm. "But I'd rather be safe than sorry." He made his way back to his tent. "Don't stay up too late, kiddos," he warned us before unzipping the flap and climbing in. "We're getting up with the birds tomorrow."

Tomorrow. The word kept echoing in my head like a song on repeat. *August fifteenth.*

I'm cold. My teeth ache. My feet ache. My chest hurts. It hurts to breathe.

Pressure on my neck. It burns. It's burning me.

But I'm so cold.

I jerk my head back. My mouth opens. Water rushes in. Mud. Weeds. Grit. My eyes hurt. It hurts; everything hurts. I can't see. I can't breathe!

I bolted upright, shivering. Sweat drenched my neck and

chest. My T-shirt was soaked and ice cold. *It was just a dream. Another dream.* I took a gasping breath and looked around. *I'm in a tent. I'm okay. I'm alive. I'm okay.* I kept repeating it with each breath, willing my heart to slide back down out of my mouth, and rehearsed all the facts.

You're alive. You're not dead. You're on a camping trip. It's Tuesday night or Wednesday morning. It's dark. You're in a tent. Chloe is sleeping next to you. Everything is sore because you portaged and canoed for a few hours. You're okay. You're fine. You just have to pee.

I lay back down, fumbling for my flashlight until the cylinder curled into my hand.

Okay. Let's just go and get this over with. Won't take long.

I unzipped the flap and crawled out, slid on my Tevas, and switched on the light. I swung it around; the weak lemony beam bounced off the bushes and disappeared into the dark. It was a completely black, starless night. Heavy clouds hid a full moon that last night lit up the campsite like a searchlight, bright enough to cast shadows.

Go find a bush and make this fast.

I crept forward carefully. I shouldn't have waited so long. I shouldn't have drunk all that Sleepytime tea before bed.

There was a dim glow through the trees—the lake. I walked a few yards on the path leading down to the beach. The stiff breeze pushed me back when I reached the narrow stretch of sand. The air felt hot and muggy on my face.

I did my business quickly and hiked up my sweatpants. I

could see better now. My eyes were adjusting to the dark, and I wondered if it was near dawn. A pink streak marked the skyline across the lake over the black furry line of trees. A strong gust of wind blew my hair back; whispering voices circled overhead. Branches swirled and sighed as the treetops bent and touched their limbs together.

The wind picked up. The whispers started to moan, then howl. I turned and scrabbled back up the bank to the trail. My feet moved a mile a minute, and after a dozen steps something thin and strong caught against my shin. I tumbled to the ground with a heavy thud. *Shit.*

What's grabbing me? I pulled my leg, panic swelling inside me like a wave, and I yanked until the tension went slack. Metal clanked on rock, and it took me another second to realize I had tripped over one of the tent lines and pulled a stake free. I rubbed my shin, feeling incredibly stupid, and then incredibly thankful I hadn't fallen on a rock and bashed my head open. *I need to be more careful.*

I crawled around to the tent opening and pushed my head in. "Chloe?"

No answer.

"Chloe!" I aimed my flashlight onto her face.

She cracked open an eye. "Wh-what? What is it? Are you okay?"

"Yes. No," I whispered. "I don't know."

"What's wrong?"

"I don't . . ." Another breeze hit my back, but it wasn't a

breeze anymore. The flaps of the tent blew in, snapping angrily.

"What's happening?" Chloe's outline rose up from her sleeping bag, and she clicked on her flashlight. "A storm?"

I nodded, then realized she couldn't see me. "Maybe."

"Should we tell Chris?"

"I think so. Yeah." I backed out of the tent and looked up. At first I thought I was seeing storm clouds—the sky was definitely lighter now, but the black and green streaks weren't clouds. They were tree branches.

This is bad. A thunderstorm? A tornado? Up here?

I scanned the other tents circling the charred logs of the fire pit. Another light clicked on. Oscar and Isaac's tent.

I watched Oscar crawl out, blinking into the beam of his own light.

"Oscar—" A sharp crack like a gunshot, like the sound of an ax splintering wood, erupted behind me. The side of my face exploded instantly with heat, like I'd just been slapped. I rubbed my cheek, smelling pine needles. It must have been a branch. I spun around but saw nothing. The wind's strength kept growing; I'd never felt anything like this before.

A hand clamped around my wrist. Chloe. "Tornado?" Her eyes swallowed the rest of her face.

"I think so." If this wasn't the beginning of a tornado, I didn't know what was.

Chloe looked up; the sky turned a sick shade of green.

"We've got to get out of here!" Oscar ran up to us. Behind him, Isaac hopped forward, trying to pull on his boots.

"And go where?" I asked, rubbing my cheek. "There are trees everywhere!"

"The lake!" Isaac ran past us. "Get in open water!"

Another gunshot. The trees groaned, bending and whipping into grotesque angles. My stomach turned watery.

Something else was coming.

I knew I should run, but my feet wouldn't move.

"What about the others?" Chloe said, her voice rising with the wind. "We need to tell them!"

A light lit up the inside of Chris's tent. "They'll be right behind us," Oscar said. "And Chris will know what to do."

The cookstove clanked and skittered past like a tumbleweed.

"C'mon!" Oscar took off in the direction Isaac had gone, and we followed. It wasn't far to the shore, and I could see Isaac already several yards out, swimming steadily. Whitecaps frothed the water around him.

"Shit! This is going to be cold." Oscar ran in with his boots on, and I followed, gasping slightly as the water soaked through my sweatpants and bit into my skin. *I don't want to do this!* I could feel my throat seizing up again, a panic reflex.

"Emma!"

I looked back. Chloe stood in the water, waist deep.

"C'mon! Hurry!" I yelled. "It will be safer out here."

Chloe stared up. "What about lightning?"

The sky was black, then gray, then green, but I didn't see

lightning. There was only wind. Wind screaming like a lunatic.

"Ow!"

"What?"

"Something hit me!" Chloe's voice sounded frantic. She quivered and rubbed her neck.

I grabbed her hand. "It's too dangerous to stay on the beach!" I tugged her forward until the water reached our shoulders. "Can you see Oscar?"

"There!" Chloe pointed her finger toward the opposite shore. "Isaac's in the middle." Her eyes met mine. "I don't see Oscar!"

I dropped my chin into the waves, fighting a familiar panic. *Not again. Not water. Not like this!* A second later Oscar's head came into view, appearing and disappearing between the waves. He looked okay. I gulped a breath and held it as a wave slapped over my forehead. *Get a hold of yourself! You can swim! You won the four-hundred-meter freestyle state championships, for God's sake. You can do this!*

"Where is everyone else?" Chloe asked, her teeth chattering. "They should have gotten here by now."

"I don't know." We held hands, but the water was so cold I could barely feel hers. The sky above us boiled with colors. Acid green and orange. Dirty purple and yellow. "I think . . ."

The sound of a runaway train drowned out my words. All around us the air flattened down, descending from the sky like an enormous fly swatter with a whistling thwack. Trees ripped from the ground and tumbled forward like bowling pins. I couldn't believe what I was seeing. There was no funnel cloud. No twister. No rain. Something sharp hit the back of my head.

"Duck!" I screamed. "Hold your breath!"

I went under and tugged at Chloe's hand until I felt her submerge next to me. *Count. Just count. Stay under. Hold your breath. One, one thousand . . .*

I made it to twenty-seven before I surfaced.

The wind was gone. Waves around us subsided into ripples, the sky overhead mottled like an old bruise. I saw Oscar fifty yards out, treading water. He stared back at the campsite with hard eyes. Amazingly, his glasses had stayed on.

"Wh-what was that?" Chloe shivered next to me, squeezing my palm. "That didn't look like a tornado at all."

"I know," I said, spitting out a mouthful of water. "I have no idea what that was." We waded back up to shore still holding hands.

"They didn't come out?" Oscar trudged up beside us.

"No." I stared at the destruction in front of us. Huge trees snapped in half and logs the size of small cars littered the slender stretch of beach. A weird blue stick poked up from the sand by my feet. A toothbrush. My toothbrush.

"This is bad," Chloe said to no one.

"I'll go look," Oscar said quietly. "You guys stay here."

I shook my head. "I'll go." I knew not seeing wouldn't help me. My imagination was always worse.

"Me too." Chloe nodded.

"Hey!" Isaac was about ten yards from shore. "Wait up!"

I didn't want to wait, not for him. "C'mon," I said to Chloe, and tucked my toothbrush in my soggy shirt pocket. There were no more trails back up from the beach, no trail anywhere at all. We had to squeeze single file through the mess, pushing over and under a fallen canopy of leaves and branches.

The campsite was gone. It was now littered with rocks and resembled a dynamite testing ground. A sleeping bag dangled from a snapped limb thirty feet in the air. A bag of marshmallows impaled by a stick, a lantern with all the glass busted out of it. My eyes glanced over a huge fallen timber, a nylon tent crushed underneath its massive trunk. But when I saw a hiking boot with the leg still attached peeking out from the destroyed tent, I realized I had been wrong.

Very wrong.

This time my imagination wasn't worse. Reality was worse. Much worse. I would never have imagined this. Not in a million years.

I exhaled as if punched; my legs wobbled underneath me. *I'm gonna be sick.* A throbbing shudder traveled from my butt up my spine, clicking my teeth together. I had somehow collapsed to the ground. Blinking, I looked up to see Oscar peering down at me.

"Emma? You all right?"

"No." My voice echoed in my ears, like an explosion had gone off next to my head. "No, I'm not."

He bent down and gripped my shoulder. "You're going to be okay."

"No," I said, fighting down the gagging sensation in my throat. "No, I'm not." *I'm never going to be okay.*

Day 3
Morning

Don't look over there. Don't look don't look don't look. Just don't.

It was like one of those weird psychological games—don't think of a white elephant. Or was it a purple hippo?

Don't think about the three dead people twenty feet away.

Dead people. But they weren't just dead people. They were Chris and Wes and Jeremy. They had families. Friends. We were their friends, even though I only knew them for two days. I needed to think about that. Or maybe I shouldn't. Maybe that was the worst thing I could do right now. To think about them as people. I didn't want to start crying. If I started, I wouldn't be able to stop. I would start screaming instead, that kind of gut-wrenching howl you see people do on the evening news. But I understood their wailing. It vibrated inside me, ready to break through at any moment.

Chloe cried. Quietly. She wiped away tears with her shirtsleeve, sniffling softly. Oscar's face alternated between shock and exhaustion. Every few steps he needed to stop and hold on to something. Isaac didn't speak, at least not as much as normal, especially after he had held up his hand when he found two bodies. Or I should say, parts of bodies.

"Don't!" Isaac's sharp voice tingled my ears. "Don't come over here."

Chloe obeyed. She sat down on an uprooted trunk, eyes blinking.

I did not.

Neither did Oscar.

But after I saw, I wished I had listened. Something pink and glistening lay in the dirt in front of us.

"What is that?" My voice sounded dangerously close to shrieking.

Oscar inhaled sharply, then covered his mouth with both hands.

"Something that's supposed to be inside someone's body," Isaac said. "Not lying in the dirt."

"We should try to find everything," Oscar suggested. "And wrap it up."

"Wrap it up?" Horrified, I stared at him, thinking I had heard wrong.

"There's a bunch of . . . *stuff* missing." Isaac waved his hands. "Do you want to go and look for it? Put it in a baggie?"

"I don't know." Oscar shook his head. "We can't leave them like this."

"Yes, we can," I heard myself say. "They're dead, and there's nothing we can do about it." I pointed at the dirty pink thing. "I'm not touching that!"

Oscar and Isaac stared at me as if *I* was the one missing my brain. Neither of them spoke.

We stood that way for a while, and I wondered if this was just another nightmare I couldn't wake up from. I was afraid to break the silence, afraid to move, afraid that this really had happened, *was* happening right now. "What about Chris?" Oscar asked finally.

Is he asking me?

"There's no way we can move that tree." Isaac crossed his arms. "It would take a bulldozer."

"Can we dig around underneath to get him out?"

"Maybe. But what are you going to dig with? Your hands?"

Oscar shrugged, mouth open, bewildered and defeated. It didn't seem right to leave Chris like that. But what could we do about it?

It was a horrific situation, but horror can last only so long. Eventually it runs out of gas, and then you're just left feeling sick and exhausted. Shaky. So tired it was like being drunk. Dr. Nguyen called it an adrenaline hangover. The aftershocks. The tremors. The headache. A physical earthquake inside—the sour stomach, snaking coils of ice, waves of sweat, a thick, swollen tongue in a dry mouth. We'd all been wandering around in circles for hours, and now the sun was up, the morning light only illuminating the disaster. Isaac kept walking around saying, "Jesus Christ." And "Jesus Mary Joseph, son of a bitch." In some way it sounded like a prayer.

But Jesus, Mary, and Joseph weren't coming. Not today.

I felt nothing. Numb and dumb. That was me—a robot. I didn't know if it was a good thing, but it was definitely a defense mechanism. I couldn't think of what to do. I had no plan.

I stared at the ground, not really seeing anything definite, just blobs of color and light. A silvery sparkle caught my eye, and I bent down. Tinfoil. A log of something wrapped in tinfoil, barely dented and covered by leaves and dirt. Food. *An enchilada*, I thought. I picked it up and put it back in the dirty cooler. *Food. I should pick up the food.* It sounded a lot better than looking for missing body parts.

Chloe slid off her stump and joined me. In twenty minutes we had gathered the following:

> A pack of marshmallows (only a few holes in the bag).
> A box of Quaker instant oatmeal (variety pack).
> Three tinfoil-wrapped enchiladas.
> A box of chocolate chip granola bars.
> A squashed package of cheddar cheese slices.
> Five bruised apples. A spotty banana.
> A tin of smoked sausages.
> A single-serving bag of Cheerios.

A fork, a tin pot with a broken handle, and a stainless-steel coffee mug (Chris's).
A half-empty bag of trail mix.
A four-pack of fruit-cocktail cups.

We walked around like that, silently gathering anything we could. Oscar picked up strewn clothing, T-shirts and sandals and plaid flannels. A pair of swimming trunks. A bottle of sunscreen. A bottle of saline solution. A flashlight. A box of tampons. A dented can of Off! Sunglasses with one lens missing. Sleeping bags. A shredded flap of tent.

Isaac sat on a stump, alternating between watching us salvage and watching the sky.

"Don't you want to help?" Chloe asked finally. She picked up a plastic comb in front of him. It was hers and she slid it into her back pocket.

"Not really," Isaac said.

"Do you always have to be a dick?"

"Only on special occasions." Isaac tilted his chin back up. "I also like to make sure that if a tree limb falls down it's not going to land on me."

That made us all look up.

I hadn't thought about that. Really, how many people do? Most people never look up, too busy with what is in front of their face.

I scanned the snapped limbs above me with renewed interest. There was a light breeze, but it was cool, not like the muggy wind from the storm. The sky was clear, a smooth and solid blanket of blue. No clouds.

I sniffed. Lake water. Ferns and pine. Cedar and moss. If I closed my eyes, I could convince myself the storm hadn't happened. Whatever it had been—a tornado or a freak wind—was gone.

"What about the canoes?" Chloe glanced from the tree-tops to Isaac's sullen face.

"What about them?"

"We'll need at least one to get back."

"Back?"

"We can't stay here."

"Yes we can. And we should," Isaac said. "They know where we are, and they'll know where to find us."

"I found one canoe," Oscar said. "It looked like an aluminum can someone stepped on." He pointed into the underbrush. "There's another one over there. But it's about a hundred feet up in a pine tree."

The kayak was crushed as well, the Kevlar hull shattered underneath the same enormous trunk lying on Chris's tent. *What would have happened if I hadn't needed to go to the bathroom?* Would Isaac and Oscar have woken us? Doubtful. I turned in a wide circle, recognizing nothing. Branches were everywhere, limbs stacked on top of each other like fallen dominoes.

Would we have been crushed? Impaled? Would a tree limb have skewered me like a human kabob? Would my skull have been cracked open like a coconut?

Stop it. Stop it now. I sat down on the cooler, suddenly hot with nausea.

"There's one more, then," Chloe said. "We need to find it."

"Be my guest." Isaac swept his arms open.

Chloe shook her head and stalked past me, muttering, "Useless."

I got back up and continued my scavenge, tugging the cooler behind me as I walked. A flip-flop. A bar of soap. A contact lens case. A stainless-steel wristwatch. It must have belonged to Chris. Nobody I knew wore watches anymore, at least no one under forty. Everybody used phones. I checked it. Still worked, ticking the seconds at a steady pace. *His family will want this. It's not much, but it's something.* I tucked it into my pocket.

"Phones." I straightened up, suddenly hopeful. "Phones."

Isaac looked at me like I was mildly insane. "What's that?"

"Where are the cell phones?" I didn't wait for his answer. "That one bag. The orange one. Waterproof, right? We need to find it."

"I've been looking," Oscar said, walking back into the campsite, his arms full of dirty and wrinkled clothes. "I haven't seen it."

"It could be anywhere," Isaac said. "It could have blown into the lake."

"No," said Chloe. "It was probably in Chris's tent."

Nobody responded. Because nobody wanted to go back over there.

"If they are," Isaac said, "they're probably destroyed."

"We should go and look."

"I did." Isaac stared at her, disturbed. "They aren't there."

"How can you be so sure?"

"I am sure."

"But you—"

"Go yourself if you don't believe me!" Isaac roared. "Go and look! I dare you."

I sat back down, feeling like I should eat something. Or maybe I shouldn't eat anything. I needed water. I wished for something a little stronger. Bourbon. Vodka. Gin. I wanted to puke. I leaned forward and pinched the bridge of my nose.

"You okay?" Oscar sounded concerned.

Do I look okay? "Mmm-hmm."

"Fine!" Chloe shouted, and stomped over in the direction of the tent. She climbed over the limb on the far side and disappeared. I tried to think about what she would do when she saw it. Scream? Faint? I didn't have to wonder long.

When someone vomits, it's a unique sound, and even though everyone does it a little differently, no one needs an explanation. Like the wailing on the news, there's not much lost in translation.

After a few minutes she climbed back over the tree and wiped her mouth with the back of her hand. She didn't look at us, and we didn't look at her. We all just stared at the ground. Thankfully, Isaac didn't say anything. No one did.

Day 3
Evening

My shadow dissolved slowly in the sand, and I when I finally looked up, only a half-light was left in the sky, fading with each passing second.

Chloe sat down next to me. "How you doing, Em?"

Em. Like my friends used to call me. Lucy always called me Emmy.

I shook my head and swallowed.

Chloe sighed. "Yeah, me too."

We looked for movement on the water. No loons. No frogs. No fish jumping the surface. Not even a bug.

"I think we've picked up as much stuff as we can," she said. "No thanks to Captain Asshole, of course."

I snorted, burying my face in my elbow. I shouldn't laugh at a time like this. Then again, maybe that was the only thing left to do.

"Did the captain decide on a course of action?"

"I guess we're staying put for now."

"Do you think anyone knows what happened?"

"I hope so. Chris said . . ." Chloe's voice cracked on his name. "He said we were remote, and we haven't seen anyone for a whole day. But you think there would be a few campsites close by?"

"Maybe Oscar knows," I said. "He was looking at the map a lot last night."

"That's what we really need to find," Chloe sighed. "The map."

"You didn't find it?"

She shook her head. "It's probably ripped to shreds, or stuck up in a tree somewhere." She kicked her boot in the sand. "Or we need a compass. Or a phone. My phone had a compass. A GPS."

"Mine did too."

The setting sun was a fireball in the sky, sinking quickly behind the trees, and we watched it turn from a bright half circle to a glowing crescent to a sliver of hot orange fingernail. "That must be west, right?"

"Yeah."

"What are you two doing?" Isaac's voice was loud. "Lezzing out?"

"You wish." Chloe flipped her finger at him, not bothering to turn around.

"Whatever," Isaac grumbled. "It's time for a powwow." He didn't wait for a reply but slipped back over a log.

"Who died and made him king?" Chloe asked. And then I immediately realized the literalness of the question. Someone had died. Three someones, actually. And our leader *was* dead.

I got up. "What happens now?"

"Maybe Captain A has a plan."

"I hope he came up with a good one."

"I doubt it." Chloe shook her head, unconvinced. "But I guess there's a first time for everything."

"I guess there is." I pulled her up; she squeezed my hand, and we walked back to the campsite in silence.

Isaac stood where the center of the campfire had been, the ground charred black under his boots. Oscar sat next to the refilled cooler and the pile of now folded clothes, and I went and stood next to him. Chloe pressed her back up against a trunk; the splintered wall of broken limbs and sticks around us made me think we were trapped in some sort of prehistoric bird nest.

"Okay," he began. "We've gathered as many supplies—"

"You did?" Chloe crossed her arms. "I thought you were just supervising."

"I was thinking."

"Oh. I see."

"And I've decided we should stay put."

"Is this gonna be a vote?"

Isaac shrugged. He clearly didn't care about being democratic. To him, this was a dictatorship.

"Shouldn't we go back?" Oscar asked. "At least to an area that's not like this?"

"We don't have a map," Isaac reminded him. "We don't have canoes. Even if we had one, we couldn't portage over that." He pointed at the wall of broken trees. "One canoe for four people? And our gear? Someone would have to swim every lake. That's hypothermia in twenty minutes."

Chloe looked down at her boots. None of us could argue with that.

"So we agree?" Isaac asked. "We stay here and wait."

"How long do you think it will take them to find us?" Oscar examined the contents of the cooler, obviously concerned with the food-and-water situation. My stomach growled.

"A day? Maybe two?" Isaac said. "It might take longer for them to get to us."

Oscar picked up a vanilla pudding cup. "Then we need to make some rules about food."

Isaac shifted his stance back, hands on his hips, studying Oscar, or more like sizing him up. I couldn't tell by his face what he decided. "You have an idea, Wiener?"

"We parcel out the food evenly. Everyone gets the same amount up front. No fighting about it."

"Sounds fair to me," Chloe said, emphasis on the word "fair."

I nodded. "Me too."

"Okay, Wiener," Isaac said finally. "I guess you're in charge of the cafeteria."

"Good." Oscar put the pudding cup back in the cooler. "Does everyone have their packs?"

Surprisingly, everyone did. Mine had been wedged under a pine branch, and it took several tugs to free it, but thankfully, nothing ripped. There were only a few scuff marks on the fabric, and although the aluminum frame was dented in places, it wasn't broken. The zipper still worked, and all my stuff was inside. I hugged it to my chest with a silent prayer. *Thanks, Dad.*

Oscar divided everything into four even piles. There was an extra apple and granola bar.

"You take it," Chloe told him. "It was your idea."

Isaac had succeeded in getting the tent up, but it must have been missing a few parts, because the roof sagged in on one side, and there was a large tear all the way down to the bottom. *Who is going to sleep in it? Are we supposed to flip a coin?*

I sneezed three times in quick succession.

"You okay?" Oscar asked, concerned. "Allergies?"

I rubbed my eyes. "It's probably dust or . . ." The taste of burned wood coated the tip of my tongue, spreading down my throat—just a small tingle, but enough to make me cough. I turned to face the breeze. Light but steady.

"Or what?" Oscar touched my hand. "What is it?"

What is it? What is it? What is it?

There was only one thing it could be.

"I think its smoke."

"Smoke?"

"I can smell it. Like a campfire." I sniffed again. "But more."

"You think?" Oscar inhaled deeply, lifting his nose with his eyes closed, like an animal trying to catch a scent.

Isaac walked the perimeter, which wasn't far, given how the fallen limbs had us penned in. "It's probably a fire," he said after completing a circuit.

"You mean a campfire?" Chloe asked hopefully.

"It *was* a campfire," Isaac said. "But now? With the windstorm?"

"Do you think it started a forest fire?" Oscar asked.

"Maybe."

"Maybe?"

I sniffed again. "What if it's coming this way?"

Isaac picked up his pack. "With our luck, it probably is."

"So what do we do? Go back out on the lake?"

"I wouldn't," Chloe said. "We have no boat."

Isaac nodded, agreeing with her for once. "If the fire does come, we'd get surrounded. And we can't stay in the lake that long. The water's too cold."

"So how do we know where to go?" Oscar's voice climbed an octave. "We'll get lost out there."

"Ouch!" Chloe rubbed the top of her head. "Something bit me!"

Isaac backed up, startled, his eyes on the trees. "Jesus fucking Christ!" The panic in his voice pulled the skin tight on my neck, goose bumps sprouting instantly on my arms.

"What's that?"

The treetops—what was left of them—were aglow with fireflies, blinking and fading in the increasing dark. But these fireflies were orange and cherry red, not halogen yellow. Giant clumps of light, like a cluster of thick snowflakes, drifted and swayed above us.

Oh my God. What is happening?

A bright orange ember turned black as it hit the ground by my boot.

"That's not a campfire." Oscar grabbed his pack and handed me mine. There was still a large pile of clothes on the ground. "Stuff as much in as you can," he ordered. "Now!"

Sweatshirts, swimsuits, a towel, flip-flops, a belt. I shoved things in without looking. "What about the cooler?"

"We can't carry that! Take the food out!" Isaac stuffed a

metal pot in his bag. "I can't fit any more in mine." When he zipped it shut, it bulged like a deformed tumor on one side.

Chloe ran past me. "It's coming! Which way?"

Smoke tickled the back of my throat. "Not into the wind." Another ember must have landed on me, sizzling as it made contact, because the skin behind my ear felt like someone had pinched it. I swore and pulled my cap down over my head.

Isaac sprinted past me and hurdled over a log, heading near Chris's tent. I didn't want to go that way, but it was the only direction we could go. Was it north? To my left was the lake. I knew we were camped on the south end, because I remembered the spot marked on the map. There were other campsites dotted around the lake; some we had passed on our way here. *How far away are they? A half mile? Two miles?* We hadn't seen anyone, but someone could be there now. *Is it their fire? Are they okay? Did trees fall on them, too? Does that mean the wind is blowing north? North by northwest? Isn't that a movie title?*

"Emma!"

I jumped. Oscar shook my shoulder. "C'mon! We have to go!"

"I know." How long was I standing there like a nitwit? "Where's Chloe?"

"She's already gone." Oscar pointed.

A wave of heat hit my back, pushing me forward. Oscar had the first aid kit strapped over his shoulder. "C'mon,

Emma! We can't stay any longer or we'll be trapped!" He grabbed my shoulder straps and tugged me forward, like a dog on a leash that doesn't want to go. I went forward reluctantly, turning my head when I heard a popping sound. A snap. *Snap. Crackle. Pop. Just like the cereal. Just like a fire. This is a fire. A campfire. A giant campfire that we're inside of. We're the meat, ready to be cooked.*

A plume of hot smoke descended over my face, searing my tongue and throat. "Oh!" I pulled my shirt over my face as I scaled the trunk to the other side, carefully stepping with my boots, hoping to feel firm ground and dirt, not a soft quivering mess of human parts. I couldn't stay here even if I wanted to. It would be horrible to burn, I realized. *Is that worse than drowning?*

"Faster!" Oscar barked. "Watch your hands! Watch your feet!"

The heat grew on my head and butt, but my pack shielded the rest of my back. How hot could something get before it spontaneously combusted? I moved faster, but it didn't seem fast enough. We couldn't run. Instead, we jumped and scrambled over fallen limbs liked panicked squirrels.

How far had we gone? It didn't seem like we were making good time, not with each of us carrying an extra twenty pounds of gear, maybe more. I doubted we could have gone more than a mile. I banged my shin against a stump, barely feeling it.

The light brightened when we stumbled into a clearing,

and the lavender sky, speckled with stars, was clear above us. Long grass waved purple-feathered tops across the field, and I chased Oscar to the center, only stopping when he suddenly pulled up and bent over, hands on his knees. He panted heavily, breathing in hard, wheezy bursts.

"You okay?" I sounded weirdly calm. We were lost in the woods, trying to escape a forest fire, and we'd just lost two people in our group. The other three were dead. We were definitely not okay. "Side ache?"

"I'm not much of a runner," Oscar heaved.

The wind was stronger in the field. I faced into it, then turned until I felt it at my back. "We should go this way." I took the first aid kit from him. "I can carry this for a bit."

I thought he might protest, but he didn't stop me when I slung it across my shoulder. "Do you think they came this way?"

"I don't know. I hope so."

Ahead of us was dark; the fire's glow behind our backs. I could hear the snapping as it ate up the ground. I brushed my fingertips over the tall grass; it would burn like straw. It would go like crumpled newspaper. "Let's go. Can you still run?"

"Jog maybe."

"Okay. Follow me." I rolled into an easy jog, heading for the dark wall of the woods. We wouldn't be able to move that quickly through the trees. "We just have to run faster than the wind." Only after I spoke the words did I realize how impossible it sounded.

* * *

We found Chloe by herself, crying.

At first I thought the moaning was the wind. Or the gasping we made as we ran, trying to stay ahead of the fire. We cut strange paths through the trees, trying to estimate the direction, sometimes stopping and turning so we kept the fire at our backs.

The moaning rose and fell, depending on the direction we moved through the trees. But one thing became certain—it was getting louder. It took me a few minutes to realize the noise was coming from a person. At least, I hoped it was a person.

"Chloe?" I threw my arm back, but Oscar was right behind me, and I hit him in the chest.

"Ow!"

"Shh." I put my finger to my lips, which was pointless. Oscar couldn't see me. I could barely see my hand in front of my face. "Listen."

Nothing. *Chloe was ahead of us. But did she go the same way?*

"I don't hear anything."

"Wait."

The sound came again. A muffled sob.

"Chloe?" I wasn't shouting, because I was afraid of waking something up, which was ridiculous. *Stop watching all those zombie shows. You'll rot your brain.* I had laughed when my mom made that joke, and she wasn't even trying to be funny.

"Chloe!"

After three heartbeats came the reply. "Emma?"

"Here!"

"Help me!"

I spun in a circle, attempting to triangulate the sound. "Where are you?"

"I don't know. I tripped." It sounded like she was trying very hard not to panic. Her voice was rough with pain. "My ankle hurts bad. I can't walk!"

"Okay!" I yelled. "We'll find you!" She couldn't be that far away. "Oscar and I are here! Just keep making sounds or something."

More quiet crying, but I still couldn't tell the direction.

"Chloe? You have to be louder so we can find you!" Oscar called. "Can you sing or something?"

"Sing?" I turned around, but he was just a faceless outline behind me. It was a good idea. A weird idea. "What song?"

"Doesn't matter."

It was quiet. Then . . .

Ring around the rosie
A pocketful of posies

We moved forward slowly, and Oscar held on to my shoulder. Chloe's voice was clear, and it grew louder, an eerie echo piercing the darkness.

Ashes, ashes, we all fall down.

Well, that's appropriate, I thought as I stepped through a pale stand of aspens, then immediately caught my foot on a clump of uneven ground and went sideways. Off balance, I pitched forward a few steps as the terrain sloped away underneath my boots, dipping down to a small ravine. This must be where she tripped. If I had been running, I would have. We must be close. I grabbed an aspen trunk to steady myself.

"Chloe?"

A dark shape huddled on the ground about ten yards away, slowly rocking back and forth. She stopped, turned her head up. "He left me."

"Who?" *Did she mean Isaac?*

"He left me," she mumbled again, more to herself. "He left me."

Oscar crouched down. "Where does it hurt?"

"My ankle." Chloe exhaled a rippled breath when Oscar put his hand on her leg.

"What about here?"

"No. Just the ankle."

"Did you hear a pop?"

At the sound of the word "pop" something fizzed and buzzed in my ears, causing my vision to narrow into a pinprick and my mouth to fill with saliva. I pressed my fingertips to my eyes and flared my nostrils. *Don't faint now.*

"I don't think so." He undid the laces and eased her boot off. Chloe sucked in a whimper when Oscar found the bad spot.

After a minute he said, "I don't think anything is broken. Just a bad sprain."

"I've rolled my ankle before. I've sprained it before," Chloe said. "But this is way worse. I can't even put weight on it."

"I know," Oscar nodded. "It's a really bad sprain. A third degree, I bet."

"How many degrees are there?"

"Three."

"So it's the worst."

"Yeah."

"Great," Chloe said through gritted teeth.

Oscar put her boot back on carefully, keeping the laces loose. "I can't believe he left you."

"I can." I couldn't help myself. "That's what cowards do," I added. *Period. Exclamation point.*

"Emma," Oscar began. "We don't know if—"

"Know what?" I was suddenly enraged. "We don't know that he's exactly the type of person who would save his own ass first?" *What kind of person leaves a helpless person behind? A gutless, worthless coward, that's who.* I bit down on my lip. *What kind of person lets her little sister die?*

The same kind.

Me.

"Lucy . . ." Something bright and hazy washed over my face, a roar building in my ears. Suddenly I couldn't see a thing.

A second later I felt Oscar grab my shoulder. "Emma!"

He shook me, rougher than I thought necessary. "What happened?"

"Nothing. I'm right here." I blinked, but the words didn't sound right. It sounded like *fight her.* I was sitting in the leaves, something damp soaking through my pants. I must have fallen down.

"Who's Lucy?"

"What?" I looked up. Oscar's pale face in the dark woods stood out, his eyes bright with worry.

"Are you all right? I can't have you spacing out on me! You need to focus."

"I am." I rubbed my eyes. The smoke had found us again. "I'm here. I'm fine."

"Okay," Oscar said. "You carry the supplies. I'll carry Chloe."

Oscar shed his supplies, and we helped her up. With three packs and the first aid kit I was loaded down like a mule, and I staggered sideways until I got the weight distributed. Now we would be traveling at a snail's pace, and if the wind picked up, there would be no way to outrun it.

Oscar squatted down, and Chloe leaned over his shoulders. "One, two, three." With a grunt they were up, Oscar looking much steadier with the extra weight than I did. "All right, lead us out, Emma."

I did, swaying and tripping forward in the dark as fast as I could, calling out hazards as I found them, and listening to the sound of the world as it burned down behind us.

I ran (more like trotted), my hands out in front of me like a blind person. But my hearing rose to the next level. The sound of crunching leaves, Oscar's heavy breaths behind me, Chloe's painful gasps.

My throat was raw, tongue swollen so it was hard to swallow. How much farther could we go? We'd been running all night. A branch jabbed my side, making me jump sideways, only to have something else poke me in the shin.

"Ow!" I stopped suddenly, leaned over, forgetting that I had three packs on me, and almost landed on my face. I turned sideways at the last second, landing heavily on my shoulder, and wound up on my back, stuck like a turtle in its overturned shell. I stared up at the hole in the canopy of trees. Bright three-quarter moon rising with wispy clouds passing across. Too bright to see stars. Or maybe the clouds were really smoke.

"Emma?" Oscar was suddenly standing over me, with Chloe's face peeking over his shoulder. "Are you hurt?"

"No," I said, and turned my head to check. "I just fell." I slipped my arms out of the backpacks and rolled onto my hands and knees. "I'm just tired," I admitted. "And thirsty."

"I know." Oscar helped Chloe slide down off his back. "Me too."

"I'm sorry," Chloe sniffed, sitting in a lump on the ground. "Me and my stupid ankle."

"It's not your fault," I said. "It could have happened to anyone." It still could, I thought.

Oscar leaned back against a tree trunk, catching his breath. "Do you still smell any smoke?"

I sniffed. "No, but I can't tell anymore." I put my face against my sleeve. "My clothes reek, though."

"What do we do now?" Chloe wanted to know. "I hate that I'm slowing you guys down."

"You're not," Oscar reassured her; he didn't say what we were all thinking. *If Isaac were with us, we'd be able to move much faster.* "We can't move very quickly in this dark anyway. There's no trail and it's too dangerous. We don't even know where we're going."

"I wish we could see the stars." My tongue was still swollen in my mouth, my ears radiating heat, my chest constricted, and sharp stabs punctured my back with every breath. I took a swig from my canteen, trying to swallow the sensation away. "We could at least find the North Star and use it as a compass."

I rotated around, looking for a breeze, something to give me a clue what direction I should take. "I don't know where we should go. For all I know we've been running in circles."

"Well, we should try to keep moving," Oscar replied, but he didn't budge from his resting spot. "We need to keep going." From the heavy sound of his words I knew he must be exhausted.

"For how long?"

"Until morning, I guess."

It would be hours before dawn. There was no way we could run or even walk all night, especially while carrying someone. "No," I said. "We don't have enough water to keep going, not at this pace."

"Then what should we do?" Chloe's voice was strained, ashamed to be the burden.

"We should find a place we can rest," I said.

"But what about the fire?" Oscar pushed off from the tree.

"Then we'll have to run again," I said. "We can take turns keeping watch, but we really need to rest. If we keep going all night, we won't have the strength to get away if it comes. We need to find a place that won't burn."

"You mean like a lake?" Chloe asked.

"Yeah," I said. "Anything near water. Or something high up, like a cliff."

Oscar agreed. "We should try to find a hill or ridge. Maybe we'll be able to see."

"All right," I said, heaving the packs back on. "Higher ground or water."

Oscar braced himself under Chloe's weight. "We'll rest more," I told him. "We can definitely do this if we take our time." I trudged forward; even I didn't believe that lie. I just hoped Oscar and Chloe would.

When the ground slanted up under my feet, I wanted to run, but by this point I was almost too tired to care. The terrain was definitely more rocky, more dirt and grit and pebbles, fewer trees and shrubs. I looked ahead, feeling something looming in front of me, but still unable to see much. "I think there's a hill up here!"

After a minute Oscar huffed up behind me. "Thank God" was all he managed to get out before sinking to the ground. Chloe hopped off his back. "Sorry." She winced. She looked at me. "How steep is it?"

"I don't know. I can't really see." And just like that, the clouds or smoke passed away from the moon, illuminating the granite ridge in front of us. It was high, at least fifty yards up, sparsely dotted with trees, and I quickly scanned the cliff face, looking for a way up. "There." I pointed to the far end. "Maybe we can get up over there."

Chloe didn't look so sure. "I can't make Oscar carry me up that."

"He won't."

"What do you mean?"

"We'll both carry you," I said, deciding the plan.

"But what about all the gear?" Oscar panted from his spot on the ground. "We can't do it all at once."

"I'll carry the packs up first," I said, "and see if I can find a decent trail. Then I'll come back down and we'll help Chloe up."

"I don't like that idea," he said. "You shouldn't do this by yourself."

"I'm not," I replied, looking down at him. "You've been doing most of the work all night. I can do this." I grabbed all three packs to make my point. "I can definitely do this."

"It's too dark," Oscar argued. "You could trip and fall."

"The moon is pretty bright," I said. "I'll be able to see better than I did in the woods." I strapped one pack to my front, the heaviest on my back, and carried the lightest one (mine) over my shoulder like a purse. If I needed to, I could drop it. I turned my head to the cliff, sniffing the breeze. *Smoke?* I needed to be fast. "Okay, I'll be back soon."

"Hurry," said Chloe, "but don't hurry. You know what I mean?"

"I do," I said, adjusting the weight. "I know exactly what you mean." I squeezed the straps tightly in my fists, willing myself a burst of energy, and started in a quick walk to the looming wall ahead. *I can do this. I have to do this.*

At first it wasn't bad. By the time I reached the rise, I had caught my breath, and the beginning of the slope was a fairly gradual incline. After a few minutes, however, the ground rose dramatically, causing me to switch to hand over foot. The pack strapped to my chest scraped against the rocks, and something inside it prodded dully against my stomach. Whatever trail there had been had quickly disintegrated. I peeked up after a few minutes, looking for the top of the ridge, but I couldn't see it. My head pounded; I was thirsty, but there was no way to reach my canteen now. Instead, I pressed the side of my face against the cliff, taking another breath before I reached my hand up, my knuckles scraping against rock. I should have worn gloves. *Did I even bring gloves?* I tested my handhold before I stepped up. So far so good. I wanted to look to see if I could see the fire, but at the same time I was terrified I might. So I kept climbing.

Hand, hand, check. Foot, foot, rest. I was almost at vertical now, and I wondered how we would get Chloe up. I would have to find a different route. This way would be impossible.

The view in front of me brightened. The moon was back out. I checked my eyes up, finally seeing the top, about twenty yards away. Small trees twisted out of the side of the rock face, but I didn't dare grab them. It was all too easy to imagine them ripping away in my hands. I knew I must be carrying at least an extra forty pounds, maybe more. I climbed more slowly, taking shorter steps, looking for handholds in easy distances. Twenty yards to go. Fifteen. Ten. Five.

Hand, hand, check. Foot, foot, rest.

I reached for a jutting chunk of granite and tugged, but the piece broke off under the pressure. My right arm flew out into space. "Shit!" I was dangerously off balance. The pack on my shoulders pulled me backward with momentum. "No!" I gripped my left fingers harder on my handhold. *Dear Jesus, please don't break. I have to drop the pack. I have to or I'm going to fall.* Still, I couldn't bring myself to drop it.

Drop it! No! Not yet! You're almost there!

Instead, I wrenched my chest back toward the rock face, using every muscle in my shoulders and stomach, while hot streaks of pain erupted under my ribs in protest. I slammed back against the cliff, the force of my impact sending a stream of gravel and sand down on my head and neck. A clod of dirt hit my face and exploded against my mouth. "Son of a bitch!" I coughed, trying not to gag. *Don't drop it!*

Suddenly I was rising, my chin butting the rocks as I ascended, like I was being lifted by a crane. Within seconds the ground flattened out, and I collapsed forward onto it and turned over, only to see a large shadow hunched over me. Isaac clicked his flashlight on, holding it under his chin. He looked like a ghoul. "You called?"

An hour later we were all huddled together on the smooth granite outcropping, taking shallow breaths through our shirts. Isaac had shown me a slim trail up the far side, steep but still walkable. Apparently I had picked the hardest route to the top. And with Oscar's help we got Chloe up the cliff. The smoke came in waves, gusting thick, then ebbing out, depending on the direction the wind shifted. It swirled so quickly it was impossible to know where it was coming from, impossible to know what to do.

So we did nothing but sit. We hunkered down, as Isaac called it, and rode it out, hoping the bare rocks would keep the flames from us.

Another gust made my eyes burn; at least it didn't feel hot. The wind seemed to be picking up.

"Thank you, Jesus," Isaac coughed weakly. He pulled his shirt down and gulped the fresh air.

"Whaddya mean?" Chloe said, her whole face buried in her flannel shirt.

"The wind's coming from the north," Isaac said. "The fire was behind us, to the south."

"How do you know?" My eyeballs felt as though they'd been scraped with sandpaper, and I squeezed them tighter, hoping to make some tears.

"I just do."

"That makes me feel a whole lot better," Oscar said. I couldn't tell by his voice if he was being sarcastic or not. Mainly, he sounded tired.

"It should. That means we won't be turning into crispy crunchies any time soon."

"Unless the wind changes direction," Chloe muttered.

"Yeah." Isaac rubbed his face, smearing soot. He looked

like he was wearing camouflage paint. "But I think we've had enough bad luck for one night."

"I think we've had enough bad luck for the rest of our lives," Oscar said.

I knew a little about bad luck, enough to know it didn't work that way, but I didn't bother to say it. There was no point. Instead, I took deep breaths of fresh northern air, grateful for the reprieve, however long it would last.

Day 4
Dawn

I woke to see the horizon edge glowing seashell pink.

How long was I asleep?

Crouched between Chloe and Oscar, I pressed my back up against the ledge and sniffed the air. No smoke. Oscar's head was crooked on my shoulder, Chloe's bad leg propped up in my lap.

"Rise and shine, sleeping beauty." Isaac poked his finger against my forehead.

"What time is it?" I wiped the crust out of my eyes, still raw and gritty.

"Time to get off this cliff and find some water." He shook his empty canteen at me. "We're out."

"I have some left." Immediately I regretted that. I certainly wasn't going to give him my share, but then again, I figured he was the type who'd just take it.

"We're going to need more soon." He kept staring at me.

Curious. Hungry almost. Like a bird looking at a worm. He leaned over me, blocking out the view, and I noticed his boots were only a few feet from the edge. If I jumped up, I had the distinct impression he would fall backward off it. Or maybe I would push him.

Don't think that stuff. My palms itched at the possibility. Chloe's leg was heavy in my lap; I knew I wouldn't be jumping up any time soon. "Chloe?" I nudged her awake.

"Mmm." She stirred, yawned, then winced. "Oh damn! That hurts." Gingerly she withdrew her leg off me. Last night Oscar had wrapped her ankle tightly with an Ace bandage he found in the first aid kit. Wedged between the layers was a chemical ice pack.

"That wasn't enough sleep," Oscar groaned softly, lifting his head off my shoulder.

"We can rest when we get water," Isaac said.

"What about the fire?" Oscar removed his glasses and began to polish them with his shirtsleeve.

"What about it? Don't matter. We still need water."

I scanned the horizon, the view growing lighter by the second. Trees, trees, and more trees, in every color green. But no blue. No silver glimmer in the distance. There must be thousands of lakes and ponds and streams out there. How did that poem go? "Water, water, everywhere, / Nor any drop to drink."

"All right," I said, heaving myself up to standing. "We should climb down to the base."

"Oh yeah, Dodd? What's your plan?"

"Well, water of course," I said, ignoring the sarcasm. "Chloe can't walk, so she'll have to stay here. Someone should stay close." I looked pointedly at Oscar. I knew if the fire came back he wouldn't leave her. "Actually, both of you should stay close." I wasn't going to come right out and accuse Isaac. That wouldn't work. I needed to flatter him—make him feel important.

"And do what, exactly?"

"You and Oscar could look for food and supplies around here. Water might be farther away."

"So maybe I should look for it."

"You're stronger," I said, trying out my version of a compliment. "And between the two of you, if the fire does come back, you'll be able to carry Chloe much faster than I can."

Isaac crossed his arms. "And what are you going to do?"

I nodded at his canteen. "I'm going to find water."

Twenty minutes later I pushed through a scraggly dogwood bush, the whiplike branches slapping thickly against my pants.

How long does it take to starve?

Two weeks without food? Ten days?

Or thirst, that's definitely quicker. Probably three days without water, maybe four.

So how do I find water?

Water was something you bought in a bottle at the Kwik Trip or ran through the filter on the kitchen faucet. Food was something you took out of the pantry or the refrigerator, something you ordered in a restaurant, bought at the grocery store. Finding those things had never been on my list of concerns.

Past the dogwood clump, the bright red berries on an evergreen caught my eye. My stomach involuntarily clenched and pulled tight as I remembered the taste of a strawberry, the sweetness bright on my tongue. When I was a kid, I once went strawberry picking with my mom and Lucy on some farm that charged by the pail. I crouched in the dirt with my little sister, and we ate them until our stomachs hurt, until it hurt to breathe. Then we filled our buckets.

But these weren't strawberries. I plucked one anyway, turning it over between my finger and thumb. *Is it poisonous?* I didn't have that book on plants that Chris had brought along on the trek. *The Upper Midwest Field Guide to Native Plant Species.* Illustrated with full-color photographs and Latin names. The first night I had scanned the pages—some of the drawings and photos from the pages on edible mushrooms— but I had skipped the section on berries. *Stupid.* The book was burned to a crisp by now, like the rest of the supplies, like Chris and Jeremy and Wes.

Probably poisonous. I flung the berry into the trees, then pulled a thin strip of plaid cloth from my down-vest pocket. Eight inches long, plaid flannel, cut from the plackets. I tied the strip around a slim white paper birch. Was the pattern called Royal Stewart? It didn't matter what it was called, only that the red tartan stood out brightly in the endless green. The shirt was a birthday present from my parents, along with a new phone. I also got art supplies from Lucy. Watercolor paints. Payne's gray, viridian, Naples yellow, Chinese white. A sable fan brush. But that was over a year ago, and I don't paint anymore.

I finished the loose knot and wiped my eyes. Two strips of shirt tied so far, at one-hundred-yard intervals. One hundred yards on a track was easy, but I was less certain of the distance out here. I had eight strips left before I was supposed to go back. The trail here was decent, made by some sort of animal, probably a deer. Definitely not a person. No one would be out this far. At least, I reasoned, not someone who wasn't crazy. Or suicidal.

It was still early, the birds shrieking morning songs in the thickets. Soon the buzz of mosquitoes would start. Another reason to hurry. I glanced up. The sun was rising steadily— already a white ball, the day promising to be hot and muggy— and I couldn't help but think about the coming snowstorm. Chris had said it was coming in a week, but what was that thing that happened last night? Just a freak of nature? Or a sign of more to come?

The weather up here, so close to the Canadian border, seemed to have a mood disorder. Clear, perfect mornings that bloomed into muggy afternoons, with blackflies buzzing incessantly. But at night the temperature dropped, sometimes by thirty degrees or more, and by the time the morning rolled back around you could see your breath as you exhaled little puffs of steam.

After another estimated hundred yards, I tied the seventh flannel strip, this one around a scraggly pine, and continued down the trail. It widened out. *A good sign? Maybe it's leading to something.* This was the third morning of the trip. No one would be looking for us until the eighth when we failed to check in. But maybe—just maybe—they were already searching, considering what had happened. I watched the sky once more, wishing for a plane, a helicopter, something. We hadn't gone more than a few miles from the last camp on foot; we couldn't be that far away, could we? They knew we were out there; they knew where we were supposed to be.

My toe caught on a rock sticking up from the dirt like a broken tooth, and I pitched forward, almost driving my face into the ground. "Dammit!" It sounded frighteningly loud in this wide stillness. The birds went silent at my outburst.

I shrugged my pack into position. *If a tree falls in the woods . . . something, something.* I forgot the rest, but I did know one thing. I could scream out here. I could cry and yell and swear my head off. I could beg and pray and plead. And I could die. No one would hear. No one would know. No one would find me. *I would disappear into the ground, just like that smushed berry I picked, just like everything else.*

A chill trickled down my back. I closed my eyes, listening. I needed to keep going. Just a little farther. *Is it "further" or "farther"?* A stupid thought at a time like this. Whatever it was, I needed to do it. I needed to find water. The canteens were empty. I took a shallow sip from my bottle, only a few gulps left. *Isn't that the clue to go back? Shouldn't I turn around now? Maybe I should have put the cloth at fifty yards, not one hundred. I should go back. What if I do fall and get hurt? I would be stuck out here.*

I pressed my hand against the shedding bark of a paper birch, closed my eyes, and smelled the breeze. *Ridiculous. You can't smell water. Can you?*

I pushed off, determined to use all my markers before I stopped. Surely there would be water somewhere. This whole forest was full of it. I should be able to throw a rock and hit it.

Keep going, I thought. *You'll find water if you just keep going. You have to.*

When I came around the corner, the trail flattened out, turning soft under my boots. Sand. *There must be something near,* I thought, and through the brush of pine, aspen, and sumac I finally saw it. Water. It glinted in the sunlight, blue and promising.

It was not a large lake, and the shoreline was sandy, studded with rocks. It wasn't one of those swampy, algae-ridden, boggy ponds, but a true lake, clear and cold and deep. I bet there would be fish—big ones. I slid off my pack, retrieved the four large empty canteens, and filled each one completely at the water's edge, promising myself I wouldn't drink any until I got back and it was sterilized. I dropped the tablets into each one—twenty minutes before they would be okay to drink. The lake smelled of weeds and iron and minerals, and the saliva flowed in my mouth, imagining how good it would taste. I splashed it on my face, running my hands over my hair. It still stank of wood smoke and burned plastic. My throat was still raw, my skin itchy. When the canteens were full, I capped them, loaded up, and headed back. Seven hundred yards to water. No problem. This would be an easy place to die, I knew, a wry smile blooming on my lips. *But not today. I'm not going to die today.*

Then again, it was only morning. . . . Anything could happen.

"You're back!"

"Of course." I shrugged off the pack and looked around. "Where are they?"

"Not far, don't worry." Chloe struggled to stand up from the log she'd been resting on, then winced and sat back down.

"How's the leg?"

"Same, maybe worse. I can't even get my boot on."

I crouched down in front of her and unwrapped the Ace bandage.

Chloe's ankle was as fat as a bratwurst. I couldn't even tell where her anklebone was, everything just inflated with fluid, the skin purpled in shades of burgundy, violet, and maroon. It looked disgusting.

"Nice." She gagged at the sight. "I look like I have gangrene."

"It's bad, but it should heal eventually. Couple days?" I wished Oscar were here. *Where did he go?* He had a better bedside manner. "I think we need some ice."

"That cold pack helped some."

"Yeah." The cold pack had eventually lost its juice, and there was one more in the kit, but I hesitated to use it. What if something else happened? I shook my head. Something else *would* happen; that was guaranteed. "I found a lake. Seven hundred yards away. If we can get there, you could soak your foot. The water's pretty cold."

"You found water?" Chloe licked her lips; they were cracked and dry like mine.

"Of course." I smiled, relieved to have done something right. "I said I would."

Chloe laughed a hard horsey laugh. "You certainly aren't like our fearless leader."

"Talking about me again?" Isaac walked in through the bushes like one of those jungle commandos. We never even heard him, and I couldn't help but flinch. He was carrying a huge bundle of sticks.

Chloe ignored his question. "What's that for?"

"Supplies." Isaac dropped them in a pile and took off his pack. "We can build a fire—"

"No fire," Chloe blurted. "What the hell are you thinking?"

"I'm thinking that if I can catch a rabbit or a grouse, I don't want to eat it raw and puke my guts out. I like my meat cooked."

"And how do you think you're going to catch a rabbit? Emma here moves faster than you."

"With these." Isaac held up a few slender sticks. "I can make a bow and arrow and some spears. That is, if Emma here will let me borrow her knife."

How the hell does he know I have a knife?

"What knife?" Chloe glared back at him.

"The Swiss Army she's been keeping in her back pocket. That knife."

I busied myself pulling out the canteens from my pack, pretending I hadn't heard him. Apparently he's been looking a little too closely at my ass. *Great.* But we did need a fire. There was a water purification kit in the emergency bag (thanks again, Oscar), but it wouldn't last us more than another two days.

"So if I can sharpen these sticks," Isaac continued, and I felt his eyes on me, "we could use them to hunt. I could definitely make a bow."

"Really?" Chloe asked, unimpressed. "How exactly will you do that? What'll you use for the string?"

Isaac crossed his arms. "Dental floss."

"Sure. Are you also going to catch birds and pull out their feathers?"

"Huh?" Isaac stared at her, his expression a mixture of confusion and vehemence.

"You know, for the end of the arrow."

"That's a good idea, though, making something to hunt

with," I heard myself say, mainly to prevent the fight that was brewing. I didn't like Isaac. But it wasn't just that; it was something else. He made me nervous. I hated the way he stared at me—part dirty old man, part disdain. And there was something mean and sharp in his eyes. He reminded me of the type of person who would drown kittens and think it was funny. Dr. Nguyen would say he was a psychopath. Or was it a sociopath. *What's the difference between them, anyway?*

Whatever he was, one thing was for sure: Isaac was unsettling to be around to say the very least.

But we needed him. Of the four of us left, only Isaac had hunting and wilderness experience. At least he said he did.

"And we will eventually need to build a fire," I said, trying not to shudder. "We don't have many sterilizing tablets left. We'll need to boil the water, and the fire could be used as a signal."

When I turned back, I saw a glimmer of hurt in Chloe's eyes. I was supposed to be on her side (I was on her side), but I also knew that Isaac was right. He smiled that triumphant, yet dirty-old-man grin at me, and I wished again for Oscar to be here. He was the level head of our group—the mediator. Nothing seemed to bother him, not even Isaac's verbal abuse.

"Where's the Wiener?" Isaac asked suddenly, obviously thinking of Oscar as well.

Chloe shrugged. "Still looking for food, I guess."

I glanced past Isaac, toward a thick copse of aspens. "I thought he was supposed to stay here."

"I told him I was fine," Chloe said. "I told him to go look for something useful."

I nodded and set the canteens up in a row on a flat stone. "These should be ready in a few minutes."

"Dodd, you actually found water?" Isaac looked impressed, or maybe just surprised.

"Of course she did," Chloe snapped.

"Seven hundred yards." I turned and pointed where I'd come from. "It's marked with my red plaid flannel."

Isaac arched a blond eyebrow and crossed his arms. "Who told you to do that?"

"Nobody." He was staring at me differently now, as if maybe I wasn't some annoying bug he would squash. "Thought it would help us not get lost. Or more lost than we already are," I added. Because we were lost. That was a fact. But we were still alive. So far. "It's a nice lake. Probably has fish. It would make a decent camp."

"Well, well," Isaac said. "Looks like you're not totally useless after all."

"Shut your face, dumbass!" Chloe snarled as she rewrapped her ankle.

"Why don't you make me?" Isaac clenched his fists. I didn't doubt he was the type of boy who would hit a girl. "Why don't you hobble over here and open a can of whup-ass on me!" He hunkered down into a ridiculous kung-fu fighting stance.

My mouth dropped open, but Chloe just started laughing. Isaac didn't seem to intimidate her in the least. "Nobody opens a can of whup-ass anymore, white boy! It's not 1995!"

"What's going on? Who's whupping ass?" It was Oscar. He looked disheveled and sweaty, as if he'd run back from wherever he'd been. Bits of twigs and pinecone pieces dusted his hair. He pushed his glasses back up his nose.

"Hey, Wiener," Isaac replied. "Chloe's just getting all north side on me. I guess I was disrespectin' her." He rummaged through his stick pile and withdrew a slender green branch. He bent it, testing its strength, then tossed it aside.

"North side, my ass," Chloe muttered. "And Emma found us water, by the way."

"You found water?" Oscar smiled and exhaled, ignoring Isaac. "Where?"

"Not far. We should go there and set up a camp." I remembered what Isaac had said. "And we should make a fire. It should be okay if we're by a lake."

Oscar nodded, pushing up his glasses again, then glanced down at Chloe. We all did.

"Yeah, I'm the gimp."

"We'll take turns carrying you," Oscar said. "All of us." He looked pointedly at Isaac, who was now busily whittling another stick with a sharp rock. *That stick looks too dry for a spear.* And the rock was too dull. A second later the stick snapped. Isaac glanced up at me, something between spite and embarrassment, then threw the broken pieces to the ground. He picked up another stick, a green one, and started again with the same piece of rock. My hand reached to my back pocket, feeling the comforting steel outline of the knife my dad had given me. *He said it was lucky. He said it saved his life.* I certainly didn't want Isaac to use it.

Chloe muttered something. It sounded like *not letting that piece of shit carry me.* Or maybe I was imagining it. It had been a day, but I didn't think Chloe was about to forgive Isaac for abandoning her when she couldn't keep up with him. She didn't strike me as the forgiving type. Then again, neither was I.

"Fine, then. Lead on, Wiener." Isaac held up the now somewhat-sharpened stick, testing it against his thumb. It looked like a squirrel had gnawed on it, but he pointed it at me anyway. "Is that water ready yet? I'm thirsty."

I tossed him his canteen, harder than necessary, a fact he didn't miss. Another thing that unsettled me about him—he didn't miss much. He gave me an evil smile while he took a swig. I should have spit in it.

"Let's go."

Day 4
Afternoon

"How is it?" Oscar asked Chloe.

"Okay, I guess."

"Better?"

"I don't know. It still hurts."

"But it's better than before?"

"Well, it's colder. It doesn't throb as much. Is that better?"

"At least we don't have to worry about alligators."

"Good lord!" Chloe jerked her foot from the water, curling her toes in fright. "Oscar! Don't even say stuff like that."

"Sorry." Oscar pushed the nosepiece of his glasses. "I guess that wasn't a very good joke."

"Can't be good at everything, Wiener." Isaac snapped another twig and put it on top of the tepee pile of kindling we had accumulated.

"Do we need more leaves? Pinecones?" I crumpled a handful

of what I thought were oak leaves, dead ones. They crackled and crunched like Rice Krispies.

Rice Krispies. Rice Krispy treats. Marshmallows. Chocolate. Graham crackers . . .

My stomach turned, making a noise that sounded like an injured animal, so loud Isaac looked up from his pile of sticks and arched an eyebrow.

"You eat anything today, Dodd?"

Why does he always call me by my last name? I guess it was better than what he called Oscar.

"Granola bar this morning." I wasn't about to complain. It was all any of us had had to eat for several hours.

Isaac shook his head. He had to be as hungry as I was, even more so. He was quite a bit bigger, and he looked like the type who could easily put away a Big Mac, large fries (supersized), plus a couple Filet-O-Fishes.

Oh God, stop thinking about food.

"And anyway," Isaac said to his pile of sticks, "there ain't gators out there, but there are snappers. Big ones."

"Turtles don't scare me." Chloe swirled her foot in the water, stretched back to catch the afternoon sun, and closed her eyes against it. It was a hot day, and her pose reminded me of the lizards in the desert, storing up heat in their bodies for when the night got cold. And it would get cold. Even in the heat I shivered, thinking about it. *Chris said a storm was coming from Canada. Maybe coming. Maybe snow.* I scanned the sky, looking for a clue, but the clouds were thin and gauzy against the blue.

"I'm not talking about those cute little box turtles you see in the pet store," Isaac replied, stuffing pinecones into the side of the tepee. "I'm talking those prehistoric big-ass reptiles. Alligator snapping turtles. Body the size of that rock you're sitting on." He pointed to the smooth granite boulder half submerged in the water. "Those things don't even look like turtles. More like frickin' dinosaurs."

"So what?" Chloe refused to let some tale of turtle terror move her, especially if Isaac was telling it. She wouldn't give him the satisfaction.

"So," Isaac said slowly, enjoying himself. "Those turtles *are* like alligators. Waiting down in the muck, looking up at the surface, waiting for something to snatch and *bam!*" He clapped his hands together with a hard slap.

Chloe snorted, but Oscar stared at Isaac, as if daring him to continue.

"Once when I was walleye fishing I saw a mallard next to our boat, about ten feet from shore. Next second I looked, it was gone. Poof! Pulled under, only a pin feather floating." Isaac wiped his mouth on his sleeve. "Wouldn't have even noticed it if I hadn't just been staring at that duck. My uncle said it could have been a muskie, but there weren't any muskie in that lake. And then we saw them come back up. Just once, just for a second, then gone." Isaac picked up his handmade spear.

"So it was a turtle?" Oscar asked, unable to help it.

"Big as a damn beach ball." Isaac nodded and turned back to me. "Think you can handle starting this fire, Dodd?"

"With what, exactly?" I asked. "Am I supposed to bang rocks together?"

Chloe snorted again. She still hadn't removed her foot from the water, but now she was staring much more closely into its depths.

"No," said Isaac, flipping me a small silver square that flashed in the sunlight as it arced into my hand. "You can start it with this."

I opened my fist. It was a Zippo lighter; a skull and cross-bones decorated one face. I flicked at the seam, enjoying the sound of that distinctive metallic *schlunk* as it popped open.

"Where did you get that?" Oscar asked. "We weren't supposed to have lighters."

"Good thing I don't care much for rules, isn't it, Wiener?" Isaac gripped his stick and turned away from the lake.

"Where are you going?" I clinked the top back down on the Zippo.

"Gonna find some dinner."

"How? What?"

"Why don't you let me worry about that."

"You know how to hunt with a stick?"

"I know how to hunt," Isaac told Oscar. "That's all that matters."

The stick looked sharp enough, and I wondered how much it would take to pierce the skin. *Not much.*

"You think you're going to be able to kill something with that?" Oscar wasn't convinced. "Just that easy, huh?"

Isaac nodded, unblinking. "Or my bare hands if I have to."

Oscar didn't reply. And neither did I. I believed him.

"Well, good luck with that," Chloe mumbled.

"Yep." Isaac walked off into the trees. "Better have that fire going when I get back. Make it smoke; maybe a plane will see it."

"I haven't seen any planes," Oscar said, poking the fire with his stick. "I haven't even heard a plane."

"Me either." I poked the charred wood with my own stick.

"Why wouldn't there be a plane, though?" Chloe asked, and pressed her fingertips into the swollen part of her ankle. It looked better, less puffy. The cold water must have helped. "I mean, I know they can't land planes on the lakes up here, right? But considering what happened . . ."

"I bet they'll come tomorrow," Isaac said, somewhat more agreeable after a shared dinner of a small tin of smoked sausages (we each got three); six marshmallows apiece; mustard, ketchup, and pickle relish packets; two squares of chocolate bar; and several shards of graham cracker.

It wasn't bad; the sausage was decent, though I usually wasn't in the habit of eating meat out of a can.

"I almost got that rabbit," Isaac said, and licked mustard off his finger.

"So you've been saying," Chloe said. "Who eats rabbit, anyways?"

"I have."

"Of course you have."

"The Germans call it Hasen," Isaac continued. "Eat it all the time, usually in stew or a casserole."

"How do you know? Are you German or something?" Chloe asked, as if that would explain it.

"My grandmother was," he said. "Spoke it a lot, too. But I'm mostly Swedish."

"Me too," Chloe nodded. "On my dad's side."

Isaac did a double take. "Johnson?"

"Yeah."

"You don't look Swedish."

Chloe just smiled as she rewrapped her ankle. "No, I don't expect I do."

Her answer made me laugh.

"What's so funny, Dodd?" Isaac appraised me across the fire. It was dusk (my mother called it the gloaming), and the light around us had a peculiar intensity that seemed to set everything aglow. Even Isaac's face.

"Nothing." I jabbed my stick at a fat coal, worrying it until it cracked apart, the inside glittering like a geode. It glowed and breathed orange light like a living thing. "Absolutely nothing." *Definitely not you.*

"So are you Swedish too?" Chloe asked.

"English, I think," I said. "Don't really know." *What does it even matter?*

"What about you, Wiener?" Isaac crossed his arms and

stared over the flames. It was amazing to me how he could make a question sound more like a threat.

"Let me guess," Chloe said. "Last name O'Brien. Irish right?"

"My dad's side," Oscar said. "My mom's Korean."

"Ah." Chloe sighed, as if that explained everything. "I was wondering why you were so pretty."

Oscar blushed. "Let's change the subject." He jabbed his stick harder into the fire, evidently uncomfortable to be the center of attention.

"All right," said Isaac. "Where you from? Johnson here is from North Minneapolis, right?"

"You know it." Chloe smiled.

"I'm from Coon Rapids." Isaac twirled a short stick point on the tip of his finger, and I wondered if he planned to turn it into an arrow.

"Surprise, surprise." Chloe wrinkled her nose.

"Yeah, I know," Isaac said. "Crapids they call it, right? White-trash ghetto, right?" He asked it good-naturedly. Having a full stomach (or at least not completely empty) had definitely improved his mood.

Chloe snorted. "You said it, not me."

"Okay." Isaac swiveled dramatically on his stump to stare at me and Oscar. "But you two haven't volunteered your information. You haven't volunteered much of anything."

I slouched over a bit more, feeling the flames bathe my face in an intense, yet pleasurable heat. "What do you want to know?"

"Well, for starters," Isaac said. "Where are you from?"

"Why does it matter?"

"It doesn't," Isaac said. "Just making conversation. Trying to pass the time."

"Fine," I said. "I was born in Saint Paul."

"I'll try not to hold that against you," Chloe said.

"But you don't live there anymore," Isaac said.

"Give up. You're never going to get it."

"I bet you're going to college in the fall."

"No."

"Really?" Oscar looked at me in surprise. Or was it disappointment?

"Community college?"

I shook my head. "Maybe I'll enlist."

"Really?" repeated Oscar.

"I might do well in the army," I told Isaac. "Don't you think?" It had crossed my mind, mainly when I saw the brochure in the counselor's office. *Be all you can be.* Whatever that's supposed to mean. *Be all what, exactly? I don't know if that's such a good idea.*

"Yeah, Dodd. I think you'd fit in just fine." Isaac rubbed his chin, thinking. I couldn't tell if he was being sarcastic anymore. Then he snapped his fingers. "I got it."

"You do?"

"You're from Wisconsin."

I opened my mouth, ready to gloat. Then I shut it. "How did you know?"

"That ugly Brewers ball cap you wear. Dead giveaway."

"Oh."

"Also, your parents had Wisconsin plates on their car when they dropped you off."

"Uh-huh," I said, and wrapped my arms around myself. It was cool now, in the night air, but I didn't suddenly feel chilled because of the weather. Creeped out, more like it. He'd noticed that on the first day. What else had he noticed? Had he been watching me? "Guess you got it all figured out. Me, anyway."

"No way," he said. "Just a lucky guess."

"We moved to Hudson a few years ago, so I don't even know if it counts." My stomach, despite the sausages and fruit cup, felt empty. So did my head. How long do you have to live in a place for it to count? Ten years? Twenty? When do you feel like you belong? Or do you never feel it? Do you always stay an outsider?

When do you feel normal again? I remembered that philosopher's quote. Nietzsche. The German guy. People said it all the time. *Whatever doesn't kill me makes me stronger.*

It sounded good, one of those inspirational quotes people liked to toss around, but Nietzsche was a liar. What didn't kill you just made you weaker, sicker, and more fragile. Little by little you started to fall apart, like a wasting disease, like cracks in a porcelain cup, like hairline fractures in your bones. The damage had been done. There was no recovery. You might have been alive, but you weren't the same. You would never be the same.

I watched the fire leap and curl, licking and eating the wood with burning tongues.

I will never be the same again.

Two hours later I found myself curled over a tree limb like something half-dead. The dinner went down fine, but it didn't want to stay down. Some kind of gnarl or knob on the tree pressed dully into my gut with each heave.

I sat up, mouth open, gulping breaths of cold night air. My throat burned from the acid, but I felt great, at least in comparison to how I was feeling five minutes ago. Clean and empty.

"You okay, Emma?"

I swiveled around and almost put my boots in the mess I'd made. I thought I had gone far enough down the shore so no one would hear me, but Oscar stood a few feet away. He put his hands up like he'd just been called out by the police.

"I'm fine. I think it was just the sausage."

"No one else got sick."

"I guess it's just me then." I wiped my mouth on my sleeve, watching him. "When I get upset or really stressed out, sometimes I get sick," I admitted. That had been happening to me a lot this past year. Even when I was really hungry, sometimes the smell or taste of something would make me sick. Dr. Nguyen would probably say it's psychological. Part of my PTSD, I guess. Needless to say, I was about ten pounds thinner than I should have been.

"Oh, okay." He put his hands in his pockets and watched the ground. "Well, do you feel better now?"

"Yeah, much," I said. "Thanks."

"For what?"

I looked up at the sky, which was clear, studded with so many stars that it looked like someone had spilled a salt-shaker in a puddle of ink. "I don't know. For asking if I'm okay, I guess."

"Oh. You're welcome."

"You sure have a way with words," I said, suddenly over-come with the idea that I should be making this easier. "What would your girlfriend say?"

"Sorry," he said. "I never know the right thing to say." He stared at me until I was certain I still had puke around my mouth. "I also don't have a girlfriend."

That's very interesting. Also very hard to believe. How could someone who looked like that not have a girlfriend? "Boy-friend, huh?" I teased.

"No." Oscar grinned at my bluntness. "I *definitely* like girls."

A flush of heat (not nausea) washed over my face. "That's what I mean." I inhaled through my nose and wiped my mouth self-consciously, trying not to stammer. "You say what you're thinking. That makes it the right thing to say."

"Oh, I don't know." In the starlight his smile looked pale blue. "Isaac always says what he's thinking."

"I think Isaac was dropped on his head as a child."

"You may be right."

I lurched myself to standing; Oscar jumped forward to grab my elbow.

"You need more water. The worst thing is getting dehydrated."

"The worst thing is I'm hungry again."

"Maybe tomorrow Isaac can spear a pheasant," Oscar said. "Or maybe hunt down a wild boar. He said he would use his bare hands if he had to." He grinned shyly and held his own up, curled forward like a monster.

I laughed, imagining Isaac trying to wrestle a pig. "Mmm . . . bacon."

"Maybe a turkey."

"Maybe a bear."

"Maybe a moose."

We walked back to the campsite this way. Maybe a fish. Maybe a turtle. Maybe a duck.

What we didn't say is what we really hoped to catch tomorrow. A plane. Out of here.

Day 5
Dawn

I couldn't sleep. My back ached. So did my stomach. We were bundled in our sleeping bags, only faces exposed, and scrunched around the fire in such a way I couldn't help but think we resembled giant caterpillars crowded on a leaf.

The fire was almost out—no heat coming off the embers. *I should get up and add some more leaves and kindling. We shouldn't let it die.* Who knew how much lighter fluid was left in Isaac's Zippo.

I loosened the bag and unzipped the side, letting in a welcome gust of fresh air. I could smell myself. Musty and unwashed, the stench of vegetables gone bad. I'm sure I wasn't the only one who stank. I ran my tongue over my teeth. Scuzzy.

I peeled the rest of the bag down to my waist, shimmied back, and climbed out, sliding on my boots, careful not to jostle Chloe. If I had slept like a baby (waking up every hour on the hour with a sudden urge to cry) then Chloe had slept like the dead. So did Isaac. Not a grunt or a snore. I know because I was awake most of the night. So much for taking turns keeping watch.

I looked over at Oscar's sleeping bag. Was he awake? He hadn't said anything after we walked back to the campsite, and he was turned away from me. His relaxed lump suggested sleep.

I should really make sure the fire doesn't die out. Having a simple, straightforward task to accomplish cheered me up, and I stepped out of the sand circle. Twenty feet away the beach dissolved into brush and trees, and I climbed through a few thickets looking for kindling. Dry leaves. Twigs. I sorted through the ones that were light and hollow. Old, dead wood. I snapped them into even pieces. It didn't take long to get a big bundle, and when I came back through the pines, Isaac was sitting up, feeding the fire.

"Where'd you go, Dodd?" The question was part whisper, part growl, but all annoyance.

"Kindling." I pointed at the obvious. "For the fire."

"I woke up and you were gone."

"I wasn't far."

"You don't wander off like that." Isaac snapped his twigs ferociously. "Not without telling someone."

I opened my mouth, ready for one of my smart-ass remarks, or better yet, one of Chloe's. *Okay, Dad.* But then I closed it. Isaac was angry; I was the reason. And something told me I didn't need to make it worse, so I crouched down into a catcher's squat. A distinct chill rose from the sand. "Sorry." The word tasted weird in my mouth; I had never been in the habit of saying it. I grabbed a pile of my twigs, twisting them together like a wad of straw, then shoved them underneath the tepee of logs.

Isaac grunted and kept shoving his own supply on the opposite side. After a minute they began to pop and snap, and the flame grew. The fire was back.

"It's starting to get light." Isaac watched the lake.

"Do you think the planes will come?"

"I don't smell any smoke," he said, ignoring my question. Or maybe he didn't know. Or maybe he did but didn't want to say. "It didn't rain last night, so the fire must still be burning, but I don't smell any smoke."

"Maybe we ran in the right direction then." I watched the flames lick up the side of the charred teepee. "Maybe it won't spread this way." The thing I didn't say was that who knew which way we actually were. Did we go north? West? In a zigzag? A circle? I shook my head; it was impossible to know. We never did find Chris's compass.

Isaac held up his hand. "No wind." He pulled the tackle box out and a broken rod (something we had been able to salvage) and started to walk out of the campsite, down toward the beach.

"Where are you going?"

"To get breakfast."

"Now? It's still early."

"Might take a while." Isaac didn't look back.

"We need a plan," I said.

He turned around and jabbed the reel at me. "This is my plan."

"Fishing?"

"We need food. We need water. Right now, that's my plan." That was the cue for me to go do something useful. There wasn't too much on the list. More wood for the fire. We had a metal cook pot that I could use to boil water in. If Isaac couldn't catch any fish—and I seriously doubted he would—then at least I could get water ready. We still had instant oatmeal. A few granola bars.

I could get wood. I could find some worms, maybe find a few fat night crawlers. Fish like to eat worms. And after I made a pile of dry logs, I would hunt along the shore and see what kind of bugs I could find, though I hoped we wouldn't have to resort to eating bugs any time soon. A plane had to come today, didn't it? We needed to make sure it saw us when it flew over.

Suddenly I knew exactly what my plan was.

I jumped up and brushed my filthy hands down the front of my equally filthy pants. Wood. I was going to need a lot more wood. I headed in the direction of a large pine, halfway up the rise from the beach, standing out from the surrounding maples like a lighthouse in a green sea. Time to get busy.

* * *

Oscar thought the raft project was a good idea, and after we made a signal flag with Chloe's pink T-shirt, we spent the next hour scouring the woods by the beach, finding the right-size logs and branches. I stared at the row of dead tree limbs, wondering how to turn it into some sort of float we could push out into the lake, something a plane would see. We planned to write the word "HELP" on it.

There were two main problems:

How to write "HELP" on a bunch of logs.

How to tie the logs together to make a raft.

"Dirt?" I suggested. "Mud? Sticks?"

"How will it show up, though?"

"Use the white aspens? We could make some mud and stick moss on it?"

Oscar's forehead wrinkles smoothed out. "Yeah, that's a good idea."

"We still need rope."

"How about we cut some fabric into strips. I have extra clothes."

I pulled out my blade, the edge dark and dull-looking. "This won't cut it."

Oscar swept his hand through his hair, thinking. "We need to sharpen it somehow."

"Rocks?"

"What kind would work?"

"I don't know," I admitted. "I don't even know how to do it."

I sat down, tired and achy. I couldn't think. "I feel like crap."

Oscar grabbed his canteen. "Thirsty?"

"Yeah." I drained the rest of my canteen, but my head still pounded.

"Where's Isaac?" Chloe asked.

"Still out there."

"Catch anything?"

"Nope. Not even weeds." Oscar sat down and tugged off his sweatshirt.

"Do you think this will work?" Chloe flexed her ankle, then rolled it in circles, frowning. It was still swollen, but the discoloration had faded. I took that as a good sign. She pulled her sock over the wrap. "Are we going to build a signal fire, too?"

Only a few wispy clouds were stretched across the blue. "Yeah, something smoky so the planes see it."

"I don't see any planes," I said.

But as I finished speaking, I heard a buzz. The vibrating hum grew behind me.

"Wait." I held up my hand, suddenly nervous. Yes. The sound got louder. "I can't believe it! I think I hear one!" Relief flushed my face.

"Get the fire going!" Oscar made a dash back to the lake, presumably to go tell Isaac.

"How do I make it smoke?" I yelled after him.

Chloe looked around. "Something damp. Something green. Something that doesn't want to burn." She hopped forward on her good foot, gaining balance. "I'll go signal at the lake." She stuck the hot pink T-shirt flag under one arm, grabbed the stick she'd been using as a crutch with the other, and vaulted herself back down the sandy trail. "Hurry, Emma!"

"Okay!" *Why didn't I think of that? What's wrong with my brain?* "Do you need help?"

"I'm good!" She hobbled around a bush, and I had to smile. Her voice bubbled with excitement. Today we would get out of here, the excitement said. Today we would go home. "You get that fire smoking!"

I fed the flames with bright yellow maple leaves. Dew-covered pinecones. Fresh green, bendy aspen branches. Chloe was right. The fire smoked. I added more, shoveling bits of damp moss in the cracks of the tepee with my stick.

The mechanical whir grew louder. It had to be a plane. As I glanced up, it passed over, white-and-silver belly flashing in the sunlight. Red-painted wings. It was a small bush plane, flying low, buzzing the treetops like a gigantic metal bug.

Smoke belched up in thick white plumes. The plane had to see it.

More pinecones. More leaves. The flames sank.

Where is everyone? I ran over to the trees; Chloe stood knee deep in the water, her sweatpants pushed up to mid-thigh, waving her pink flag like a bullfighter. Despite not being able to walk, or maybe because of it, all her energy pulsed out of her arms and shoulders.

I looked farther down the shore. Oscar was running, waving his hands like Chloe, but Isaac didn't move. I squinted, watching him cast and reel in the line. *Does he even know what he's doing? Why did he have to go halfway around the lake to fish?*

The sky was quiet. Would the plane make another pass? I could hear my blood pound in my ears. That was all. *Did it see us? It must have seen us. It had to have seen us.*

"Dodd!"

I turned away from Chloe's flapping pink shirt dance. "What?" *How long have I been standing here?*

Isaac clutched his tackle box to his chest, his reel trembling in his hand. He was breathing hard, probably sprinted the whole way back. "What are you *doing?*"

"Making the fire smoke." I gripped a clump of moss in my fist and looked down. No red embers left at the base.

Isaac dropped his stuff. "Smoke my ass! You put the damn thing out!"

"It'll come back," Oscar said, trying to calm him.

"Dammit!" Isaac ran his hand through his hair. It stuck straight up. He jogged back into the trees to find dry wood.

"I was trying to make it smoke," I told Oscar, my face flushing. Isaac had the amazing ability to make me feel like an idiot.

"Well, you definitely succeeded," Oscar said.

A plume of mossy smoke hit my face. "Do you think they saw us?"

"I hope so. I'm sure they saw Chloe. That shirt is pretty bright."

"So now what?"

"I guess we wait." Oscar looked at me expectantly. "The plane will probably radio back. It can't land up here."

"Do you think they'll send one of those boat planes that can land in the water?"

"Maybe. But this lake might be too small to land on."

I narrowed my eyes. The widest part looked almost four hundred yards across. Surely a small plane could land on it?

Oscar kept watching me, then he held out his hand.

"What?"

"How much food do we have left?"

"Not much. Only the oatmeal. Maybe a little pickle relish and mustard." My dizziness returned. *Probably inhaling too much smoke.* I turned away before Oscar cut in. "I'm going to go get Chloe and see if she needs any help." I took my time on the walk down to the beach, my boots shuffling slowly in the sand, and filled my lung with breaths of clean air. In a few seconds the dizziness was gone, like it had never happened. Here and gone. *Just like the plane.*

"It's been hours."

"Three."

"It's been three hours."

"I know. I just said that."

"I hope they're on their way."

"I'm sure they are."

"Because it's been hours."

Oscar and Chloe kept recycling this conversation. But I understood it. It was hard to be still or quiet; the silence pressed around us like an invisible wall, punctured intermittently by a bird chirp.

I watched the raft as it drifted listlessly toward the center of the lake, and only now, from this distance, did I realize how small and pathetic it appeared. If a plane did fly over, would they even see it? Would they recognize it for what it was? I squinted fiercely, unconvinced, and sighed. All we wanted to hear was another plane, but it was like that old saying my mom was fond of, the one about watching a pot that doesn't boil. So Chloe kept talking, her way of not watching, as if the more we pretended not to notice, the faster things would happen.

The afternoon dragged, regardless. Isaac didn't want to listen to us, so he went back to "fishing," which meant he moved his spot even farther down the shore.

Thinking about the possibility of fish increased that dull stabbing in my stomach, so I concentrated on poking my stick in the fire. *All we have left is oatmeal. How long can we go without food before we get too weak to function? Too weak to try to hike out. A few days?* I had hardly ever gone more than a few hours without something to eat, let alone a few days.

I turned over the small charred pieces with my stick, stirring up the embers. The light smoke kept the mosquitoes away, and I took that time to sit down and check for ticks. I peeled down my socks. Nothing on my ankles, but those little black deer ticks were the ones I was worried about and the hardest to see. Where I lived, Lyme disease was scarier than influenza.

When I was done with my examination, I peeled off my flannel and shook it out, sending waves of dust and grit into the breeze. It stank of smoke; I should wash it. I should wash myself. Rubbing a palm down my hair, I was certain I could grease a cookie sheet. I hated feeling like this, sour and dirty. I would have made a horrible pioneer.

"Where's the soap?" I asked.

"I have it." Chloe dug a square green plastic case from her pack and snapped it open. "It looks brand new." She sniffed it. "What's that smell?"

Oscar took a whiff. "Old Spice."

"Yuck."

"Well, it's probably better than what I smell like," I said. "I definitely need to use it."

Oscar tugged his shirt away from his chest. "I think we all do."

I looked at him. His face was streaked with soot, his hair disheveled in a way that some people spent a lot of time and money to achieve. If anything, he looked better than he should, and my face grew hot as I caught myself staring at the ring of dirt on his neck.

"This is all we got." Chloe tossed me the case and grinned. "Don't drop the soap."

"Yeah." The bar was a swirl of red and white. It did smell like Old Spice, definitely better than smelling like sweat, smoke, and BO. I wondered if it would wash my clothes as well as my body.

"There's a little beach over there." Oscar pointed in the opposite direction from where Isaac had gone.

"Oh. Okay, thanks." I didn't like the idea of Isaac and me sharing a beach, and I hoped it would be far enough away that he wouldn't be able to see me, at least not any detailed images. I certainly didn't need to put any ideas into his head.

I shook my own, resigned to the knowledge that they were probably already in there anyway, grabbed a towel, and headed down to the shoreline.

I trudged along the sand until I reached a spot that was wider, almost like a small half-moon inlet. The water was clear. No weeds or sludge that I could see, and smooth pebbly rocks studded the sand. This was probably the best it was going to get, so I got undressed (but kept my underwear on) behind a leafy dogwood and debated whether I should wash my clothes. I had a pair of sweats, a couple of T-shirts, a down vest, underwear and socks, and of course my red flannel shirt with half the bottom cut off. I also had a pair of quick-dry Columbia pants that zipped off at the knee, the ones I was currently using.

I pulled my hair out of the bun. Despite keeping it pulled back, it was a snarly mess, hanging in greasy lank waves past my shoulders.

I slid on the only surviving pair of flip-flops, and with a bottle of shampoo in one hand, the soap in the other, I slowly waded into the lake, gritting my teeth. It was cold. Not freakishly cold, but cold enough so it hurt.

Just get it over with.

I dropped down, submerging myself. Underwater I gasped. When I stood up again, my skin was glowing pink, and my heart was beating like a jackhammer. The water cascaded down my back in a sheet, making me feel strangely happy. I quickly washed my hair, both the bottle and bar of soap floating next to me, and scrubbed my skin until it felt like a layer was missing. Even though I knew I was contaminating the water, I was too dirty to worry about it. Surely one bath wouldn't hurt? I peeled off a sliver of soap with my fingernail and used it to wash my clothes. Then I rinsed everything and my wad of clothes, turned, and swam back to shore.

"Hey, Dodd." Isaac smiled, wolfish. He leaned against a pine tree like he owned it, holding my towel. "Whatcha wearing?"

I crouched down so the water hit my chin. "What are *you* doing here?" I asked, trying to keep my voice even. "I thought you were fishing."

"Fish weren't really biting." His smile slid wider across his face. "And I thought maybe I would take a bath, but someone took my soap."

"Here." I tossed the soap at him from my squat, but it hit the sand at the water's edge. Isaac walked forward and picked it up. "Now give me my towel."

"Done so soon?" He pulled off his T-shirt suggestively. "Want to wash my back? I have some sweaty crevices I can't quite reach."

"I'm good. I'm done. I want my towel." My teeth chattered on the last word.

"You cold, Dodd?" Isaac held up the towel, then snapped it away. "It's a bit nippy out. This is so nice and dry. Maybe you should come and get it."

That's what he wanted. Maybe to embarrass me. Maybe to scare me. Maybe to make me cry.

I'm not going to play this game.

"Okay." I stood up and let the water pour off, and clenching the sodden wad of clothes in my fist, I waded up to the beach.

Isaac at least had the decency to step back and get red in the face when I took the towel from him. His filthy smile was gone too, replaced with a glazed expression, which was a much better look on him.

I wrapped the towel tightly around me and handed him the bottle of rosemary shampoo. "Don't use it all up," I said. He nodded, swallowing hard, and as I walked back to camp, I could feel his eyes on me. But I wouldn't give him the satisfaction of turning around.

Day 5
Late Afternoon

The storm started like a headache. First the sky dulled—a veil of gray erased the blue. White cumulus clouds bloomed on the horizon, inflating like balloons, pushing the air in a new direction. The breeze shifted and cooled, and a few minutes later a branch of halogen light spread a web of electric fingers across the newly darkened sky.

"Now what?" Chloe asked as we watched the clouds pass lightning back and forth. "I hope it's not like last time."

"I don't think so. It looks different." I counted eight seconds before the belching rumble broke over us. Did that mean eight miles away? Was that far? It looked like it was coming this way. "I think it's just a regular thunderstorm."

"Will the plane come back?"

"Maybe they can't fly in this."

Chloe sighed. "Great."

With the sun gone the breeze was almost chilly. A raindrop plopped onto the sand. Then another.

"Where are the boys?"

"Trying to catch fish, I think."

"Trying. Trying," Chloe muttered. "I'd rather have oatmeal."

"Me too." We each had two packets left, and none of us had eaten it. Not yet. That was the last resort.

The fire sizzled. Rain was coming. "Let's pick up the sleeping bags," I said. "We need to keep our stuff dry."

"But where?" Chloe looked around the small site. The trees were wispy and thin on the beach, providing no cover.

"Back in the woods." I rolled up my bag and cinched it tight. Chloe did the same. Then we did Oscar's and Isaac's. "We might have to move deeper into the trees. Get under some cover or something."

"I don't know." Chloe's voice wavered. She was thinking of what the trees could do. So was I.

"It's not like last time," I said, trying to convince her. "That's not going to happen again." I shoved the last of my things into my pack.

"You don't know that."

"You're right; I don't." I looked back to the water. Oscar and Isaac were jogging back, but I couldn't see if they had any fish. "But I do know I don't want to sleep in a wet sleeping bag."

"But what if the plane comes back? They won't see us."

They're not coming back. Not in this weather. Who knows how long it will last. "We need to stay dry."

Something in my voice must have swayed her, because she hobbled forward on her crutch and picked up her jacket. I grabbed her pack just as Oscar and Isaac came up from the beach.

"Catch anything?" I asked.

"It's going to rain," Isaac said, not answering me, which I guess, in a way, was an answer. *No.*

"Thanks for that, Captain Obvious." Chloe crutched her way around the sand, up to the thin trail that climbed into the trees.

"No," Isaac said flatly. "I mean, it's really going to rain." He jerked his thumb up. "Those are some big-ass thunderheads."

Oscar grabbed his gear and looked around. "We got everything?"

"Yeah," I said. "Everything that shouldn't get wet, at least."

"Now where?" Oscar looked back at the clouds, which seemed to be multiplying like bacteria. The sky was the color of lead.

"I saw a big pine back over there." I pointed over Isaac's head. "It was really thick. Branches went all the way to the ground."

"Good." Isaac started walking that direction. "Let's get under it."

Chloe crutched up next to me. "What about lightning?"

"It'll be okay." Oscar tried to reassure her.

"What if lightning hits the tree?"

"It won't."

"But what if . . ."

"I don't want to play that game." Isaac spun around viciously quick. "It's a waste of time! It won't help, and it doesn't matter." He stepped forward, agitated. "What if we do get hit by lightning? What if a tree falls on us? What if there's a forest fire? What if we get lost? What if we die?" He pointed his finger in her face. "I hate to break it to you, sistah! We're already up shit creek without a paddle! Literally!"

Chloe's brown eyes glimmered with angry tears. I knew that look. For the past year I had had that look—two seconds away from crying.

"Shut up!" I screamed at him. "Shut up, shut up, shut up!" Even though everything he said was true, and even though everything he said made sense, I boiled with bright-white hatred. I wanted to punch him in the face.

His sneer was as quick as a snake. "What was that, Dodd?"

"You deaf?" I gripped my bag like it was a grenade I couldn't let go of. I could barely believe what I was saying. I didn't even recognize my voice. "You heard me."

"I did." His eyes were violent blue. "I just wanted to make sure I heard you correctly."

"You did." A gust of wind came with the rain, spattering the lake with a thousand pebbly drops.

He clenched his fists at his sides. *C'mon,* I thought. *C'mon and do it. Show everyone how tough you are. I know you want to.*

I stared at his hands. *Will it hurt? I've never gotten hit in the face before. Will it break my nose? My jaw? Will my teeth go flying? How much blood will there be? Will I lose consciousness? Will I have a brain hemorrhage and die?*

"Knock it off, Bergstrom," Oscar interrupted, his voice dangerously quiet.

"Make me!"

"Okay." Oscar stepped forward. "I will."

"Don't make me laugh, Wiener." Isaac looked momentarily confused, possibly because no one had accepted his challenge before now. His eyes flickered over Oscar with uncertainty. "What? Are you gonna do some weird kung-fu shit or something?"

"Yes." Oscar didn't smile. "How did you know?" I couldn't tell if he was serious or not. Thankfully, neither could Isaac. He tilted his head to the side and blinked, his mouth puckered up in disgust.

"What the hell are you smiling at, Dodd?"

"Huh?"

"You're smiling like a loon." His fists relaxed. "You look crazier than a shithouse rat."

"Maybe I am."

"Well, you're definitely something." At least now the sneer was out of his voice.

The rain pattered down, and if we didn't move, we'd be soaked in a few minutes. "Why don't you go find us that pine tree you were talking about," Isaac ordered.

"It's right through those trees, up that rise." I jabbed my finger at him, enjoying the effect, which was him immediately turning around to follow my directions.

I touched Oscar's hand, my thumb to his. "Thanks."

He looked startled for a second, then smiled. "No problem."

"So do you know kung fu?" Chloe whispered, impressed.

"No." Oscar grinned, nodding at Isaac's retreating figure. "But he doesn't know that."

Despite the rain, I couldn't stop smiling.

"Don't worry," Oscar reassured us as we headed up into the woods after Isaac. "It will probably pour for a little bit and then clear up."

I followed, not caring very much that I was getting wetter by the second, but I probably should have, because as it turned out, Oscar was half right. It did pour, and it did eventually pass through and clear up. The next morning.

Waves of fog steamed up from the lake. When the downpour finally stopped, sometime early morning, I noticed how clean and green everything smelled.

One problem: The raft was nowhere to be found. We'd have to make a new one.

"It probably sank in the storm," Isaac said, not sounding the least bit upset about it.

"Do you think it put the fire out?" Oscar pushed his way out from under the rain-softened pine needles. Despite being fully covered by the branches, we were soaked.

"If that didn't put it out," Isaac replied, "I don't know what will."

My socks squished in my boots with each step. I had barely slept last night, but for some reason I was wide awake. I felt like I'd just drunk a pot of coffee, which reminded me that even though we were soaked with water, I was incredibly thirsty. I licked my lips and grabbed my canteen. The rain-storm had filled it, and it took all my willpower to just take a few sips. Thankfully, I wasn't hungry. At least not yet. Maybe I was getting used to subsisting on five hundred calories a day. Maybe it was like some kind of high that dieters chased after, like I heard happened to long-distance runners.

"I'm starving," Chloe said as she crawled out on her knees. "Do you think the fire really went out?" she asked me.

"I hope so." I picked up her dry pack. Oscar had placed the ripped piece of nylon tent over our packs to keep them as dry as possible, and I'd also watched him fall asleep with Chloe's bad foot in his lap. He had told her it would be better if she rested with it elevated, and even though I knew he was right, her appreciative smile had bugged me, and I had turned away, shuffling around the wide base of the tree so I wouldn't have to look at them. But my pack had been soaked through on one side, the place where the tent fabric didn't reach. I kicked a rock, annoyed.

"Emma?" Chloe blinked innocently, her eyes big with concern.

"I'm fine." *Well, no, not really.* I sighed, fatigue settling back down over my shoulders, and my stomach churned out a rumble. So much for thinking I didn't need to eat. "I'm just tired. Didn't sleep much."

"Yeah, I heard you." Chloe nodded and adjusted her crutch. "You were mumbling or something. Sounded like a nightmare."

"I was?"

"Yeah, you kept saying the same thing over and over. Louder than you usually do."

Louder than I usually do? The rumble in my stomach dropped. She had noticed. She had heard me. But I didn't remember having a dream. "What did I say?"

Chloe frowned. "Uh, I don't know. Didn't really make any sense. I couldn't really understand it."

My nightmares were back. But this time it was different. This time I didn't wake up in the middle. This time I couldn't remember it. I thought they were gone, but maybe I've been having them the whole time and I just didn't know it. Maybe I was getting used to them. What's the word? Desensitized. But I had no idea if that was a good thing. Not likely.

We hiked back down to the beach. The sand was like wet cement, the campfire circle now a sodden mess of black sticks and leaves. Oscar started restacking the ring of stones, a pointless attempt to tidy it up, but it wouldn't help until everything dried, and who knew how long that would be.

"Do you think there's any dry wood around?" Oscar plopped a round stone on the sand.

"Nope." Isaac shook his head.

"Maybe we should look anyway."

"Go ahead. I'm not wasting my lighter trying to set fire to something that won't burn."

"Then how will we boil the water?"

"We won't." Isaac wasn't going to be a helpful problem

solver today—that much I could tell. He didn't even turn around to acknowledge us. He just watched the lake.

"How much clean water do we have left?" Oscar placed a flat rock on the top stack of the ring. The fire pit did look better now, but Isaac was right. There was nothing dry enough to burn.

"All the canteens from last night are full," Chloe said. "So I think if we conserve it, it should last through the day."

"Good." Oscar smiled at her, sending another pinprick of irritation under my jaw. *Why do I even care? I barely know him. I barely know any of them.*

"How many water tabs do we have left?"

"Four."

"That's not enough." Isaac turned around and crossed his arms. "That's only good for a day for all of us."

"Well, that's what we have left," Chloe said.

Isaac grabbed his canteen, the battered tackle box, and the rod. "I'm going fishing," he declared, as if that wasn't already obvious.

"That's all you do," Oscar said, somewhat under his breath.

"We *need* food," Isaac growled back.

"What are we supposed to do?" Chloe lowered herself gingerly to the ground, elevating her foot so it rested on a log. She was taking Oscar's advice seriously: rest, ice, compression, elevation.

"I don't care," Isaac said. "You can sit there and pick your butt if you want."

"I thought you wanted to be in charge."

"Nope. You must have confused me with someone else." He jogged off before she could reply.

I unzipped my pack and found most of my clothes were wet. Everything stank like mildew. "Dammit."

"What's wrong?" This time Oscar was asking.

"Nothing!" I said, much sharper than I intended.

"Are you sure?"

"Yeah." I knew I sounded just like Isaac, and I wondered if bad tempers were contagious. I pulled out a wet clump of shirts. "I'm going to find a place to dry this."

"Oh, Em," Chloe said, tightening the wrap on her ankle. "Your stuff got all wet."

"I guess there wasn't enough room for all of our stuff under the tent." A mosquito bit my neck and I slapped it, causing me to drop my clothes. Even better. I stalked off before Chloe and Oscar could say anything, following Isaac's lead.

I didn't go far, and it didn't take long to find a knobby branch to drape my clothes on, but I took my time and walked far enough so I didn't hear the others, until I found an open patch in the canopy where the sunlight filtered through. I sat down and waited. At least my Columbia pants were almost dry, but my underwear wasn't. *I should just go commando. Not like it matters.*

My stomach was really burning now, plus I was thirsty. What were we going to do even if Isaac did catch something? Eat it raw? Sashimi wasn't really my favorite.

Desperate, I dug around in my pack until my hand closed on something smooth and round. When I pulled the apple out, I was momentarily confused. I had already eaten my piece of fruit. Oscar was the one who had the extra apple; I remembered him putting it in his pack after we had divided everything up. He had somehow put it in my pack when I wasn't looking.

I hung my head, closed my fist around the apple, and let the hot tears come out. *My face is raining.* That's what Lucy used to say when she was four years old. If she pinched her finger or stubbed her toe or banged her arm by accident, hard enough to make her cry, she would say that. *My face is raining, Emmy.*

I'd wipe her tears with my palm and calm her down. *It's okay, Lucy-goosey,* I'd tell her. *The sun will come back out soon.*

I ate the apple, right down to the core. Then I ate the core, saving seven teardrop-shaped seeds. I dug shallow holes with a stick. Seven holes for seven seeds. Maybe one would live and sprout into a tree. One by one, I planted them in the sunny patch and covered each seed with a scoop of dirt. When I finished, I sat back and closed my eyes against the sun, feeling desperately tired even though I hadn't done a thing, watching the sun move slowly overhead, shadows following, growing shorter until they vanished. It must be midday.

By this time my clothes were mostly dry, with the exception of my wool socks. I moved them around as the light changed, turning them over, repositioning them to hang from other branches when the occasional soft breeze came through.

Still, it was too humid (even in the shade), and I was sweating again. I really needed to drink my water. But then what? My canteen was half empty, and even if I drank the rest right now, I would only want more.

I slapped my legs. At least a dozen new mosquito bites decorated my ankles in a bracelet of puffy white and pink lumps.

"Hey, Dodd." It was Isaac. "Keeping busy?"

I tried not to flinch; it seemed to be a talent of his to appear out of nowhere, without making a sound. I swallowed my startle in a quick gulp. "Doing laundry."

"Right." Isaac set down his tackle box and rod next to me. I didn't look up; I imagined he was staring at me again, but this time he actually knew what I looked like without my clothes on. I made an X on one large bite with my thumbnail. Isaac cleared his throat suggestively, and that's when I finally looked up and saw the fish. There were two—big fat ones with shiny olive-green skin decorated with golden pebbly spots.

"Oh my God!" I said, jumping up, my itch forgotten. *Fish! Fish! Food!* Still, I couldn't stop myself from shouting the ridiculous question. "What is that?"

"Northern pike, I think." Isaac grinned, vindicated, and held them up with some effort. "The rainstorm must have stirred them up from the bottom or something." The line strained, close to snapping. "I think this is almost five pounds total."

I salivated, fantasizing about how good it would taste, until I remembered we had no fire. "How are we going to cook it? All the wood is wet."

"Yeah, but I think if I can get it hot enough I can get some of the smaller pieces of wood to go. We just need to find one dry log somewhere."

"But how will you get it hot enough?"

Isaac's blue eyes were sly and glinting. "I only need some paper."

I scuffed my foot in the dirt, dejected. "Well, I don't have any."

"Wiener does," Isaac said. "I saw him reading a book the first night. I think he has a few of them."

I was momentarily disgusted about using a book to start a fire. Then I got over it. "Do you think he'll give you one?"

"Probably not," Isaac said. "But I'm sure he'll give it to you."

I remembered how I had stalked off this morning and felt my face redden. "I wouldn't be so sure about that."

"Then make him." Isaac was suddenly in front of me, his hand encircling my wrist, hard and solid as a real handcuff. His breath was hot and sour in my face. "Make him," he repeated. "I've seen the way he looks at you."

"Stop it." Ice-cold waves flooded my stomach. "Let go of me."

"Or what?" Isaac's clear blue eyes turned hazy. "Or you'll

scream? Go ahead and scream." His grip tightened.

I pulled away, but he just followed, pushing me backward until I was pinned up against a tree. He wedged my legs apart with a knee and hiked me up, scraping the back of my head against the bark.

"I don't mind screamers," he whispered.

I couldn't speak. It was as though he'd also pinned my throat shut.

"What's the matter, Dodd? Cat got your tongue?" Black pupils swallowed up the blue, and he pressed his face closer. For one horrifying moment I thought he would kiss me. "Maybe we should do a rerun of that beach scene from before." With his free hand he pulled the strap of my tank top over my shoulder, teasing me. "Nice," he purred. "Though you're a little skinny for my taste."

I couldn't let him see I was afraid. *That's what he wants.* "I bet," I finally managed to spit the words out. "I bet you say that to all the girls."

He leaned back and looked me up and down, but I refused to blink. "You're funny, Dodd." He grinned, quick and evil. "I like that." Suddenly I was sliding back down; he'd let go of me, and I almost collapsed when my boots touched the ground.

"Thanks," I breathed, almost choking on the word. *You're not funny at all. You're crazy. You're a goddamn psycho.* I pulled my tank top strap back up, suddenly relieved he hadn't torn it. How would I explain that to Oscar and Chloe?

Isaac swung his fish over his shoulder, giving me an innocent smile. "Remember what I said, Dodd. I'm counting on you." He whistled as he walked back to camp, the same tune I'd heard him do before, but it wasn't a happy melody, and it took me a moment to finally remember where I'd heard it before. It was a year ago, at my sister's funeral.

"What do you mean you want to burn my book?"

"I don't *want* to burn your book. I *need* to burn it."

"You said nothing would burn. All the wood is wet." Oscar put his hands on his hips. "Or did you forget that part?"

"I didn't forget." Isaac pointed to the pile of recently filleted fish. "Look at them! If I don't cook them soon, they'll rot."

"But how?"

"I need a small fire. I need some paper. We can't let this go to waste!" Isaac's voice pitched high, taking on a new urgency. I felt it tremble in my throat. We were all hungry—and I knew if it got bad enough, I would eat the fish raw. Worms and salmonella be damned. I would eat it raw. If it came to it, I would use my bare hands.

"Did we even find a dry piece of wood?" I'd rehearsed the question several times in my head. Still, my voice wavered. After Isaac's threat, my fear of him had doubled. Tripled. Before, I thought him a jerk, but now I realized I had no idea what he was capable of. One thing I did know—being hungry made him even worse.

Isaac nodded. "Two logs I found back in the ravine on the far side of the lake. Barely rained on."

"Okay," Oscar said, doubtful. "Then why do you need my book? Just start the fire."

"Christ, Wiener!" Isaac ran his hand through his hair. "I said barely wet. I need something dry that will catch right away. I don't know how much fuel the lighter has left."

I'd already piled the least damp pieces of kindling into a tepee, and I knew I needed to convince Oscar. "We need to cook that food. We need to boil water." I put my hand on his arm. "And we need a signal fire. We *need* a fire, period. The searchers need to know where we are."

Chloe agreed. I knew as soon as I mentioned searchers she'd be on board. All day we had waited for the sound of a plane, but the sky so far remained silent.

Oscar dug into his pack and pulled out the paperback. "I haven't even finished it." He handed it to me, just like Isaac said he would. Actually, it was more like he slapped it into my hands.

"Thanks." I looked at the book, then at the ground.

"Whatever," he muttered.

He was pissed. *Is he mad at me?* "I'll just take the pages from the front."

"It's not very long. There aren't many pages."

I glanced at the cover. *Hatchet.* I had read it as a kid. I thought everyone had, and I said as much.

"No," Oscar said. "I never read it. I thought it would be a good story for the camping trip."

"What's it about?" asked Chloe.

Isaac shrugged. "Who cares?"

"It's about a boy named Brian," I said slowly, watching Oscar's face. I guessed that since he was halfway through it he knew exactly what it was about. "He gets stranded in the wilderness, but . . ."

"But what?" Chloe grips her hand tight to her crutch.

"But then he realizes no one is coming."

"What?" Isaac asked, suddenly interested. "But he survived?"

"He had a hatchet. It helped him survive." I flipped through the pages, thinking about my knife. My grandfather's knife. *He said it saved his life.*

I closed the cover, pressed it between my hands, and then handed the book to Isaac. He took it without a word and began tearing out pages one at a time, as delicately as you can rip a piece of paper. The sound of it burned my cheeks.

"I'll buy you a new copy when we get home," I told Oscar. His face now had the pinched look of someone who'd just been slapped.

"When we get home," he agreed. His voice was hollow; he didn't believe me. For the first time since the accident I felt a sharp needle of doubt. *You're not going to survive. Not this time. You cheated death twice. You shouldn't even be here. You don't even want to be here. Now you're going to die. I hope you're satisfied.*

Two people died in the car accident. Three people died in the storm. But not me.

Not me, not me, not me.

All this time I'd been wondering why I had lived. I was looking for an answer that didn't exist. There was no reason. I was just like Brian, only without a hatchet. But I did have a knife. And I also wasn't alone.

Isaac already had the fire started. He gave me a look—did it mean I had succeeded? That I'd done what he wanted? That he wouldn't threaten me again?

My questions grew with the flames, until only one remained, burning in my brain like the fire. One I couldn't answer, one nobody knew the answer to, least of all me.

Who was going to survive this time?

Day 6
Sunset

There was one plane that flew low over the trees that afternoon, a duplicate of the one that had passed over yesterday, but unfortunately we hadn't made a new raft. It wasn't a floatplane, and I realized Oscar was right. This lake was too small and narrow for a plane to land on. They'd have to get to us by foot.

"Which direction did it come from?" Oscar asked. "South? East?"

"I don't know." I pointed over a giant spruce. "From there, I think."

"Do you think we should try to hike back?" He glanced at Chloe, who shook her head.

"The last thing we should do right now is try to hike back there." Isaac kept himself busy feeding twigs into the small flames. "You saw all those logs piled on top of each other. Some of them were over ten feet high. It'd be like climbing through a giant Lincoln Logs booby trap."

Without another word Oscar turned and walked back to the beach.

Chloe gave me a look: *Now what?*

I followed the trail down to the lake. Oscar stood with his back to me, arms hanging limply at his side as he watched the water, which was the same shade of blue as the morning glories my mom grew every year along our backyard fence. Morning glories were Lucy's favorite, the ones called Heavenly Blue. They usually bloomed on her birthday. There was not a better color. There was not a better name, and I briefly wondered if my mother had planted them this year. I doubted it.

"They're probably searching for us right now," I said finally. "They probably have it all mapped out. They'll go lake by lake. We wouldn't want to try to hike to a place they've already covered."

"So you think they'll just find us here?" Oscar stared up at the pink streaks in the sky.

"I bet they're on their way. It will just be hard to get to us. They'll need chainsaws and . . ." I stopped. I didn't know what they would need to find us.

"But what if the fire's still burning?"

"If it's not big, they just might let it burn," I said. "Or they'll put it out. It will just take longer."

Oscar's eyes were bright and shiny behind his glasses when he finally looked at me. "How long is long?"

"They know we're out here," I said. "They won't give up. I know."

"Do you?" Oscar sank down into the sand and crossed his legs, elbows on his knees.

I sat next to him. "Do you think they found the campsite?"

"I hope so. Then they'll know."

I was quiet for a minute, letting a horrible idea take shape, an idea I'd forced away until now. Rescuers finding the obliterated campsite, then the bodies. Broken trees, everything in charred lumps. Would they even be able to identify them now? Chris? Wes? Jeremy? "What if they think we're already dead? All of us."

"Don't say that." Oscar looked ill.

"Sorry." I wrapped my arms around my knees and hugged myself. "I can't help it."

"I know." He exhaled. "Just don't say that to them."

"Why not? I'm sure they're thinking the same thing."

"They can think it. Just don't say it. Saying it makes it real." Oscar looked back at the water, the heavenly blue color tarnishing to silver before our eyes. "We can't panic. We need to stick together."

Apparently he thought Chloe would flip out, and Isaac would leave us. Both were definite possibilities, and I didn't want to deal with either of them. If anyone was going to make it out of here alive, it would be Isaac. He would do whatever it took. That fact made me shiver.

"Okay," I said. "Don't panic. And then what?"

"And then we just keep doing what we're doing. Technically

we aren't even missing. They have search-and-rescue squads up here. They have rangers."

I scooped up a handful of dark sand. "We need to get Chloe's ankle better."

"Yeah, we do," Oscar said. "But that kind of thing takes time."

"You know if they don't come for us . . ." I stopped and corrected myself. "If they don't find us, we'll need to leave." The sand trickled through my loose fist slowly in a steady stream, like an hourglass timer. "At least try to find a trail or a campsite or a ranger station. Something."

"I know."

"We can't stay here," I remembered Chris's words when he told us about the coming storm. *Better to be safe than sorry.* "There could be a snowstorm in a few days. We need to move."

"How's the foot?"

Chloe wriggled her toes, then carefully rolled her ankle in a clockwise circle. "Much better." She smiled, relieved. "So much better."

Isaac had decided smoking the fish would take too long, so now he was boiling the pieces in the pot. I had heard of fish boils, and though I preferred mine fried, I'd take whatever I could get.

"You should probably wash that bandage while you're at it," he said. "It smells like ass."

"Well, I guess you would know," Chloe said. "You're the expert in that area. You probably have a PhD."

Isaac grinned back at her wickedly. "Yeah. They call me Dr. Ass because I get so much of it."

"Hoo!" Chloe screamed. "Is that right? I thought it was because you're so full of shit."

Oscar covered his face with his hands, his shoulders shaking up and down.

Isaac pointed his stick at him. "What are you laughing at, Wiener?"

"Nothing."

Isaac shoved the stick back into the pot and speared a white piece of flesh. "You should never laugh at people who cook your food."

"I'll remember that, Dr. Ass."

"I mean it, Wiener."

"All right. Let's go to the beach, Chloe." Knowing what I did, I really didn't want Isaac to get mad again. Chloe wasn't the type to back down. Oscar was the mediator, but I didn't know exactly what type I was. Maybe the change-the-subject type. "We won't be gone long," I said.

Isaac waved his stick in lazy circles at me. He looked like he was planning something, and it probably wasn't something good. "Just be back in time for dinner, kids."

I was overcome with the urge to warn her about Isaac, but I waited until Chloe and I got all the way down to the beach. What would I say, exactly? That he gave me the creeps? That was obvious. Or should I tell her what had happened? The thought made me hot and suddenly nauseated. What would she say? Or, more importantly, what would she do? Tell Oscar? Confront Isaac? I wasn't sure I wanted to find out, and even though I knew we were out of earshot, I whispered when I spoke. "Maybe you shouldn't push him like that."

"What do you mean?"

"You know what I mean," I said. "Like *that*."

"Mmm." Chloe pursed her lips and looked at me sideways. "Not my fault I have better insults."

"Yeah, but I think we should be nicer." I shuddered again, remembering the pressure of his knee between my legs as he pinned me against the tree like a bug.

"What for?"

"What do you think would have happened to us if Isaac hadn't caught that fish?"

"You probably would have."

I thought about that. "I didn't remember to grab the rod and reel and tackle. Isaac did."

"Yeah, right before he ran off and left us."

I remembered what she had said when we found her that night. *He left me. He left me.* "What happened out there?" I asked, louder than I intended.

"I don't know." Chloe shook her head, either not wanting to tell me or really unsure. "I just know he's a jerk."

He's more than that, I thought grimly. "Come on," I said,

wringing the bandage dry. My hands were so cold they hurt.

I gave Chloe back the bandage, my hands throbbing, and shook them to get the blood flowing. *And this is the warmest the water is probably going to get. What are we going to do when the weather turns?*

So far all the days had been extremely warm, warmer than average, but the image of snow covering us as we slept popped into my head. We had no tents, only sleeping bags. "We need to make a shelter."

"Huh?"

"You know, like a hut or something. In case it rains again." What I didn't say was *in case we are out here for a while.*

"A hut?" Chloe pulled on her tank top, then her waffle-weave thermal shirt, and topped it off with a navy blue hoodie. We'd all taken to dressing in layers. I could have used a ski hat, mittens, and a scarf. Maybe one of those bala-clava things. During the day it was fine, but the nights were cool, almost chilly.

"Yeah." I chose my words carefully. "This morning when I woke up, I could see my breath."

Chloe nodded. "I actually read a wilderness-survival handbook after I signed up for this. They said most people get into trouble because of two things: exposure and dehydration."

"Well, we got the hydration part okay. What else did it say?"

"Oh my God!" Chloe yelled.

"What's wrong?"

"Not what's wrong! What's right! I can't believe I forgot!"

"Huh?" I had no idea what she was talking about. There didn't seem to be anything right.

But Chloe was already crutching back toward the trees, hobbling along like a drunken peg-leg pirate. "C'mon! I'll show you!"

"This! This is what I forgot about!" Chloe tugged a small black zipper almost hidden on the underside of her pack. When it opened, another layer extended like an accordion, expanding to reveal a second compartment. "I can't believe I forgot." She pulled out an orange nylon bag, just like the one Chris had put our cell phones in. "It's a survival kit."

"What?" Isaac jumped up, almost knocking over the pot. "You forgot? How could you forget something like that?"

"I got this backpack at the last minute. I was going to use my old one, but it wasn't big enough."

"Huh?"

"What's in it?" Oscar asked, his face brightening with hope. It was a nice thing to see.

"I don't even know." Chloe opened the kit. "My uncle Jimmy gave it to me. He was in the army. He's the one who loaned me his pack. He just said, 'There's even an e-kit on the bottom.' At the time I didn't know what he was talking about."

"An e-kit?" I wondered out loud.

"Uh-huh," Chloe snorted. "I guess it stands for 'emergency.'" If she was embarrassed, she didn't show it.

"Your uncle was in the army?" Isaac's question was almost a whisper.

"Yeah," Chloe said. "In Iraq. First Gulf War. He's retired now, though."

"My dad was too," Isaac replied, staring at his hands. "Medically retired."

"Open it up." *Please let there be food.*

Inside, the contents were displayed in their separate compartments. A plastic whistle. A waterproof matchbox with wood matches. A small mirror. A small first aid kit. An insect head net. A plastic water bag. Four food packets. A miniature LED flashlight. A tiny tube of sunscreen. A bundle of wire. Iodine tablets. A thin foil blanket. A candle. A compass.

Oscar grabbed the compass, delighted. He held it out straight armed and turned in a circle, watching the dial to find north. He stared. He turned. He looked at it and shook it. "This is broken." He shook it once more to make sure.

"Let me see." Isaac flipped the compass around in his hand and frowned. "Must have gotten crushed or something."

Chloe unfolded the tinfoil sheet. "This is a body sheet, I think. It can keep us warm."

"It's only big enough for one person," I pointed out.

"We can take turns using it," Oscar said. "Or just save it for whoever needs it most."

"Or we can all zip our bags together and cuddle." Isaac

gave me a quick look before he handed me the compass.

It had indeed been crushed. The red needle never wavered, no matter what I did. "Actually, I was thinking we should build a shelter."

"You were thinking again, huh, Dodd?" Isaac slid the bundle of wire into one of his zippered pants pockets. "Don't strain yourself."

"What's that wire for, anyway?" Oscar asked, giving Isaac a hard stare. He hadn't missed the look Isaac had given me. Oscar was too smart not to notice, and I wondered briefly if he knew what Isaac had done on the beach with the towel. *He doesn't know what Isaac did to me. What would happen if he knew?*

"Snares."

"Snares?"

"That's what I said." Isaac palmed the matches as well. "Don't you know what a snare is, Wiener?"

"It's a trap."

"*Sí. Tú es muy correcto.*"

Is that supposed to be Spanish?

"So you know how to make one?"

"What do you think?"

"I think no," Oscar replied and crossed his arms.

Isaac laughed. "You're right; I don't. But then again, that never stopped me before." He turned on his heel, heading toward a thick grove of jack pine. He unraveled the wire as he walked, leaving us to enjoy our newfound presents. "Have fun building your log cabin."

Day 6
Night

After Isaac left with the snare wire, we started on a shelter with the entrance facing the beach, but an hour later it still didn't look like much, more like a fort a bunch of little kids would make, if that bunch of kids were all slightly drunk.

We stacked aspen limbs on top of each other to make a wall positioned to face the woods. Oscar and I did the same on each side, using sharp rocks to dig a foot-deep trench in the sand to support the wall, which eventually got about four feet high.

"Now the roof?" Oscar wiped the sweat from his neck.

"Give me a minute." I sat down, exhausted. My palms were burning and itchy with sap.

"Maybe you could lay the thin leafy branches over the top," Chloe said, taking a break from her whistle blowing. Oscar had told her to stop. She'd been blowing it every five minutes, and now my head was ringing like I'd been kicked. "Those pine ones are nice and wide."

"Yeah." I rubbed my hands together, trying to remove the oily resin. "But we don't have a hatchet to cut the branches. Too bad there wasn't one in the emergency pack." I remembered Oscar's book. *Brian survived with just a hatchet.* I shook my head. *If Brian had been real, he would've ended up dead.*

Oscar gave me a look, and at first I couldn't figure out what it meant, but then I realized I'd been talking out loud. Like a crazy person.

It was almost dark when we finished, but Isaac still had not come back.

Chloe alternated between watching the woods and watching the fire. The whistle hung low around her neck, and she played with it absently. She peered inside the shelter's entrance. "So are we all going to fit?"

"It's wide enough if we all sleep in a row," I answered, "but who's gonna sleep next to Isaac?"

"I'll pass." Chloe screwed her face up like she'd caught a whiff of something rotten.

Even Oscar wrinkled his nose, considering the possibility, then looked at me.

What would Isaac do if I were curled up next to him? "Not me!" I yelled. "No way, no how, no thanks."

"Maybe we should draw straws."

"Or pick a number."

"That's stupid."

"I pick eight." Isaac stepped into the circle on the opposite side. "Eight's my lucky number."

The bright glow of the fire made the woods behind us invisible, and a person could sneak up on you that way. It's like someone looking into a house with all the lights on inside at night. They can see you, but you can't see them, watching from out in the dark.

How long has he been standing there?

Long enough.

"We built a shelter," Oscar explained.

"I see that." Isaac curled up the remaining wire into a tight circle around his wrist, and I guessed by his face that he hadn't caught anything. "It looks more like a pigpen." He stuffed the coil of wire back into his pocket. "Then again, a pen has four sides, so I don't know what the hell that mess is supposed to be."

"It's better than nothing."

"Thanks, but no thanks," Isaac replied slowly, looking at each one of us in turn. "I'm not sleeping in that."

He grabbed his sleeping bag from where it hung on the low branch of an ash tree. It was thinner than mine, I noticed, obviously worn, and I doubted its warmth. Mine was rated to ten degrees below zero, insulated with some weird material NASA probably invented, but what kind of crazy person would want to sleep outside in that kind of weather? By contrast, Isaac's didn't look much warmer than a flannel sheet.

"Here," I said suddenly. "Use this." I tossed the folded thermal wrap at him and he caught it, but not before I saw his face. A look I recognized. Once I thought it was embarrassment, but now I knew it for what it was. Shame. He turned away without thanks.

What did he hear me say? Doesn't matter. Just don't piss him off. Don't even give him a reason. People like Isaac always seemed to be looking for exactly that, any excuse to explode.

I turned away and crawled into the shelter.

Why am I in the middle? At least with only the three of us I had plenty of room.

Oscar had zipped the two thickest bags together—making them into a giant pocket we had to slide into. Since mine was still damp, it was hung above us across the top, anchored on each side by flat rocks. It only covered about a third of the shelter, but I had to admit it was warmer here, if not slightly claustrophobic. But if it rained again we'd still get soaked. *What if it snows?*

"Snug as a bug in a rug," Chloe joked as she eased herself in.

"Hey, Wiener," Isaac called out, his voice sounding very close. "What's it like to finally have a threesome?"

"When I do, you'll be the last one I tell," Oscar replied.

"Touché, Wiener!"

"Perverts," Chloe snorted. She turned over on her side and in ten seconds seemed to be asleep.

I couldn't understand how she could fall asleep so quickly. I stared up at the sky, which was not a sky of stars at all, but a dark shadow of cover. Every cell in my body was awake, a fuzzy tingling of anticipation I thought I'd lost. But here it was again, and I didn't know whether to be relieved or guilty.

My entire body thrummed with that energy, feeling myself so close to Oscar that my breath caught in my throat as though I had choked on it.

And Oscar turned toward me, the heat of his body pressing against my own. "What is it?"

Say something. His face was only inches from mine. I could just move into him. *Just move. Just move.*

I tilted my head forward.

"Holy shit!" Isaac screamed.

I sat up. We all did, the three of us rising up like puppets on a string.

"Sonsabitches!"

It's just a joke. He's just messing with us. But my body didn't agree, and I didn't think Isaac was that good of an actor. It was something. Something big.

Still, I sat there motionless, fighting the tingle in my legs.

Oscar pushed the bag off, crawled out the opening, and flipped over on his side, like a soldier exiting a bunker that's under fire.

"What is it?" Chloe grabbed my arm. "What do we do?"

Chloe couldn't run away. Not yet. The whites of her eyes glowed in the dark.

"Stay here." I dug into my pocket and retrieved the knife, pulling open the longest blade. "Use this if you need to." It looked pathetically small, but Chloe curled her hand around it appreciatively. "Give me your whistle."

I crawled out the way Oscar had—forward on my elbows, toward the lake. Once outside I still didn't hear anything. I rolled onto my side, panic doing strange things to my body. My head felt light and empty, but my legs were lead weights.

Get up. Get up. Get up and move.

I crouched behind the wall of logs and peered over. The fire was steady, and Isaac stood in front of it, staring over the flames. Oscar was next to him, crouched down like a catcher behind home plate.

I stared, only seeing a solid wall of black beyond the fire.

Then the black moved.

Oh my God, what is it?

I blew the whistle—hard. The shrillness pierced my eardrums like a hot needle.

Branches shuddered and snapped, sending the leaves moving back and forth like a massive black wave. Something large was moving out there, and I could only hope that it wasn't coming this way. It rolled past us, and in the glare of the fire, all I could make out was a dark hulk of something crashing through the bushes.

"Emma!" Oscar grabbed my shoulders and pulled me back, but I barely heard him. I was blowing the whistle with everything I had. "Get back!" He flung a large rock into the dark.

"Shit!" Isaac yelped. "What is *that*?"

I spit the whistle out of my mouth as Oscar flung a stick in the same direction as the rock, and I waited until I heard it crash to the ground. "Something really damn big, I guess."

"You guess?" Isaac stared at me, but I couldn't tell if he looked pissed or amazed. "Why the hell did you blow that whistle?"

"I don't know. I thought the noise would scare it away." I took another shaky breath and held it.

"We don't even know what *it* was!"

"I think it might have been a bear," I said. I couldn't really think of another animal that was that big, except maybe a moose. At least I hoped to God it was an animal.

"That was a stupid thing to do! What if you pissed it off?"

Oscar spun around and glared at Issac. "What would you have done, oh mighty hero?"

"I'll tell you." Isaac considered the question. "I think I would have shit my pants and hoped the bear was so disgusted he wouldn't eat me."

Chloe popped her head out of the shelter. "Do you think it'll come back?"

"Better not."

"If it thinks we have food it will," I said. "It probably smelled the fish."

"I cleaned off the log with boiling water." Isaac crossed his arms in defiance. "I'm not stupid."

It's not your stupidity that concerns me. "Well, it's probably hungry. And it might come back."

"Then we need to do something," Oscar said.

"Like what? It's not like Johnson here can walk."

"Why don't you mark a perimeter then?"

"How?"

"You know how. You know, mark your territory."

"You mean like you're trying to do, huh, Wiener?"

"I don't know what you mean."

"Of course you don't. Besides, I don't have to go right now."

"Why? Did you already piss your pants?"

Still shaking, I crawled back in by Chloe. I gave her the whistle, and she handed me my knife.

"I can't believe you did that."

"Me either."

"Why did you?"

"I don't know." I shrugged, glad she couldn't see my face in the dark.

"I wish I had your confidence."

I pulled the cover up to my chin. "Most of the time I don't."

Chloe patted my hand. "Could've fooled me."

"Hey, ladies." Isaac stuck his head through the entry. "Room for one more."

It wasn't a question. We shuffled closer together, and Isaac crawled in on the opposite side, next to Chloe. Her teeth flashed a wicked grin at me in the dark when Oscar crawled in next to me. His hand brushed my elbow, running up the length of my arm, and though it may have been an accident,

I decided to take it as in invitation. After all, we could die tonight. We might very well die tomorrow.

I grabbed his hand and rolled toward him, burying my face against his shoulder. His body stiffened in surprise, then relaxed in such an easy way it felt like we had done this before, and his other hand curled securely around mine. Neither of us spoke; I didn't look at his face and enjoyed the feel of his chin resting on the top of my head.

"We'll take turns keeping watch," Oscar said into my hair. "In case it comes back again."

We all agreed to take a shift, starting with Isaac.

It was a good plan, a fine idea, but every single one of us stayed awake until dawn.

Day 7
Afternoon

The plan was this:

Boil enough water to fill the canteens.

Climb a tree.

"Climb a tree?" Oscar furrowed his eyebrows at Isaac. "What for?"

"So we can see where the next lake might be. And if there is any smoke from the fire."

"It would have to be a really tall tree," Oscar said.

"I know."

"How tall?"

"Tall," Isaac said.

"I'm not climbing a tree."

"You afraid of heights, Wiener?"

"No. Not abnormally."

"What does that mean, *abnormally?*"

"It means that I don't have an abnormal fear of heights,"

Oscar explained. "I have a normal fear. All people are born with a normal fear of heights."

"Why do you always have to sound like such a smart-ass?" Isaac sneered.

"Better than being a dumbass."

"Touché, Wiener. Touché."

"All right." Chloe was getting sick of their conversation. "So let's say we do climb a tree and see a lake. So what? How do we know that's the direction we should go?"

"Well." Isaac raised his eyebrows. "That's the million-dollar question, isn't it? If we go east, eventually we'll hit Lake Superior."

"That's probably at least fifty miles away," Chloe said.

"More than that, I bet."

"Yeah, no problem."

"Well, we'd probably find people or something before that."

"Says you."

"I wish we had a compass that worked," Oscar muttered. "Or a watch. Then we could find south."

"What do you mean?" I asked. "Why would that work?"

"I was talking to Chris about it the first night," Oscar explained. "I asked him how many times he'd been out here. Said he used to go camping all the time by himself, and I asked him if he'd ever gotten lost."

"Well, did he?"

"No," Oscar admitted. "Said he always had a compass and

a map, but then he pointed at his wristwatch and told me that if something happened and he lost those things, that he could still make a compass out of his watch."

"Are you sure?" Chloe narrowed her eyes. "How?"

Something turned over in my head. Chris. A watch. A fuzzy whir started at the front of my forehead. Something. Something. What was it? I was still tired, still lethargic, but something turned me around. I headed over to my backpack. The bottom inside pocket. *Where is it?*

"He showed me," Oscar said, squeezing his eyes shut to remember the instructions. "It didn't really work because the sun was already setting, but he showed me how you did it. He said you just needed a sunny day."

"Well, we got that," Isaac replied. "You remember how to do it?"

Oscar nodded. "I just need a watch."

"Here." I grabbed Oscar's hand and put the watch in it. I curled his fingers over it. "So let's see it."

"Oh my God!" Chloe said. "You had it all along?"

The way she said it made it seem like a bad thing. "I found it, yeah, but I had no idea about the compass thing." I swallowed, nervous. "I thought maybe his wife or family would want it back. If he did have a wife or family," I added quickly. I turned to Oscar, who still looked a bit stunned. "You didn't tell me about the compass thing."

"I know," he said slowly, and slipped the watch on his wrist. He looked up at the sky.

"All right, Wiener." Isaac crossed his arms. "Let's see it. Find us south."

"Why south?" I wanted to know.

"That was the other thing he told me," Oscar said softly. "That you should always try to head south, at least up here anyway. He said that if you did that, eventually you'd find a road or a trail. On the map the road ran east-west, so if you kept south you'd eventually hit it."

Chloe nodded. "I'm so glad you talked to Chris."

"Me too."

"Chris never told me that," Isaac protested, sounding more than a bit defensive. "And we spent a whole afternoon fishing together."

"Did you ever ask him?"

"No, why would I do that?" Isaac crossed his eyes at him.

Oscar sighed. "Okay, if I remember correctly, he said you had to find the sun, line it up with the hour hand like this." He stretched his arm out and turned, and I saw that it was a few minutes after one.

"Then what?"

"Then I bisect the angle between the hour hand and the twelve to get the direction."

"What do you mean, bisect the angle?"

"It means cut in half."

"I know what bisect means," Isaac huffed. "But why?"

"That becomes the north-south line." Oscar turned again. "So the line is here, between the twelve and the one."

"Okay," I said, not really getting it. I looked at Chloe—her face was open, curious, something forming behind her eyes.

"So then," she said, somewhat excitedly as she did a slight turn with Oscar. "This would be south." She pointed into the trees, and I wondered if that was the original direction we had come from. It seemed right.

"Are you sure?" Isaac looked disgruntled. "How do you know it's not north?"

"Because when Chris drew a picture in the sand, the S was at the top of the line, and the N was at the bottom," Oscar explained. "I think you do it differently if you're in the southern hemisphere."

For one second I understood, and then it was gone. "Well, it sounds like a good plan to me."

Isaac crossed his arms, unmoved. "I still say we should find a tree. We should head east to Lake Superior."

"Okay," Oscar said. "Go find one and climb it. But I just found south."

"You're forgetting one important thing," Isaac sneered.

"What?"

"South is the direction we came from, and I don't know about you, but I'm not going back into that hellhole."

Day 7
Sunset

"Are you ready?"

"I guess," I said to Oscar, folding my swimsuit into a small wad. We'd spent most of the afternoon sitting around while Isaac fished but caught nothing. "Not like there's much to pack."

"Yeah."

I slowly carved another slash on the tree trunk with my knife. Day seven was over, which meant the storm was another day closer. When I glanced at Oscar, he was watching the sky, no doubt thinking the same thing. We knew we couldn't stay here, and we'd waited long enough. "Isaac said we'll leave as soon as the sun comes up."

"Makes sense."

"Yeah." I flipped the blade down and put it away. "Sorry I didn't tell you about the watch."

Oscar shrugged. "You couldn't have known."

"Well, I should have brought it up. We could've have been home now if I had." I didn't really think that was true, but it seemed like something I should say. I had thought it, anyway.

"No." Oscar was adamant. "We did the right thing, coming here. We did everything we were supposed to. And if they were going to find us, they already would have."

"Do you believe that?"

"I have to," he said. "Otherwise I would make myself crazy, second-guessing everything all the time."

I gave him a wry smile. "Welcome to my world." I turned my eyes back to the lake, taking it all in. "I wonder what this lake is called. It seemed like every one had a name."

"Yeah." Oscar scratched his chin, now shaded with stubble. "Loon Lake, Mud Lake, Star Lake, Snowflake Lake."

"Snowflake?"

"I think there was one called Christmas Lake, too."

I tried to visualize the map—the multitude of blue splotches scattered across the green. Names and names of water. It seemed as though everything had a name, everything was known and marked. "Well, this one's really small."

"Tiny Lake?"

"Doubt it."

"How about Lost Lake?"

"Good one."

We watched the sun disappear over the trees, leaving a golden glow in the sky.

A long cry shot up over us, so close and high and lonesome

it made every pore on my skin contract, like a shock wave starting from the deepest part of my gut.

"What was that?"

As if to answer the question, another cry echoed some distance away, but the effect of the sound was the same. I felt the tingle all the way to my butt. "Wolves." I exhaled. "It's wolves."

I'd heard the sound before, of course, in movies and nature shows, but out here it was different. This wasn't a movie, and it wasn't a zoo. It was the wild. This was their home; we just happened to be here.

They appeared on the far bank, between a clearing in the trees, moving as smoothly as ghosts, their long-legged strides so even and fast they appeared to drift and hover over the ground, not touch it. I counted three. They were slim and lithe, brushed in various shades of gray and white, moving quickly down the shoreline, their eyes and noses missing nothing. The last one in the line stopped and turned its head to us, examining the strange creatures on the opposite shore. Had it ever seen a person? I hoped not. And I hoped that after tonight it would never see another one of us again. It tilted its head up, another moaning cry rising like the beginning of a warning siren, and a few seconds later a fourth wolf burst from the south end of the lake, running in a steady lope to catch up. They nuzzled at each other for a second, turned, flicked their tails, and were gone, disappearing back into the trees.

I grabbed Oscar's hand. "They were right there. So close."

"I know." He squeezed my hand and, with one quick tug, pulled me against his chest, wrapping both arms around me. I couldn't say what shocked me more, the wolves or his embrace, and I almost forgot where I was. All I could concentrate on was the feel of his body against mine. Another howl echoed through the sky, making me shiver. "It sounds closer now."

He watched the trees. "Do you think they'll—"

"Yes." I exhaled, not letting him finish, and we turned (somewhat reluctantly) and ran for the campsite.

When we burst back into the clearing a minute later, my heart was pounding so loud in my ears I barely heard what Chloe was telling me, or rather yelling, her mouth compressed into a frightened O.

"Wolves!"

"I know! We saw them!"

Isaac was already growing the fire, the biggest I'd ever seen it, but he added several large logs around the base, cursing frantically when his hands got too close. "Wiener!" he yelled. "We need more! They're coming!"

I stared into the trees. The light was gone, the view growing dimmer by the second. I half expected them to leap out of the bushes any minute. How long would it take for them to come around to this side? *Immediately*, came the answer. Not long. Not long at all.

I jumped when Chloe grabbed my arm. "C'mon, help me."

She tugged me to the shelter, and I saw she had already covered the top, making a solid roof of crisscrossed branches of pine and poplar, woven together with geometric precision. My face flamed. I'd been talking with Oscar while Chloe had been fortifying our shelter.

"These!" She pointed to several large limbs stacked next to the hut. "Help me move them in front of the entrance."

A minute later there was only a hole big enough to squeeze through. I took off the top limb and tossed it inside. "Do we have any sticks?" I yelled, but Oscar was already next to me with a handful.

"We can make spears with these if we have to." He pushed me to the entrance. "Get in now!"

"What's Isaac doing?"

"Trying to get the fire higher. It needs to last all night."

Chloe had already climbed in, pulling all the packs inside. She pressed them against the walls as fortifications, and now it resembled a crude bunker.

"They're coming," I said, praying I was wrong, but at the same time strangely excited. "He needs to get in here now."

"I know." Oscar looked back at Isaac, who was hurriedly dumping dry leaves and twigs into the fire in the hope the big logs would catch. "Isaac! Leave it! C'mon!"

The warning in Oscar's voice made Isaac jerk up. He glanced around quickly, then jogged over to us, apparently as nervous as we were. He had never obeyed a command so fast without an argument.

We climbed in through the hole, and when Isaac was in, he stuffed the opening shut with the last log.

Chloe hunched in the corner and clicked on her flashlight. She pushed her back against her pack and held the sticks for dear life.

I pulled out my knife and crawled over to her. "Here," I said. "We need to sharpen them to spears."

The shelter was even more cramped with all our gear inside. Oscar took his pack and leaned it against the opening. Each one of us took a side. Through the cracks in the wall I watched the woods behind us, hard to see anything over the height of the fire. If the wolves were coming, they'd be coming from that direction.

"Now what?" Chloe handed Isaac a sharpened stick.

Isaac took it eagerly, then turned his attention to the darkness beyond the glow of the fire. "Now all we do is wait."

We didn't wait long.

They arrived like a fog, so silent and smooth that for a moment I didn't understand what I was seeing. Eyes. Golden eyes appearing, then blinking off, like a short in a light circuit. There then gone. The eyes moved but didn't get closer. I held my breath and stared, hoping I wasn't hallucinating. Then I hoped I was.

"I see them," Chloe whispered. "Back there."

"Me too." I gripped my stick tighter. "But they're just sitting there."

"They're waiting," Isaac said grimly.

"Waiting for what?"

"For the fire to die."

Oscar exhaled hard and leaned heavily against my back. I pressed my shoulders against his. "I thought wolves didn't attack people," he said.

"A pack will," Isaac told him. "Especially if they're hungry."

Especially if they're hungry. Yes, I could see that. To wolves we would be easy, much easier to catch than a rabbit or deer. Much easier to bring down than a moose. Despite being called the most dangerous predator on earth, humans were a pretty pathetic specimen, physically speaking.

"How many do you think there are?" Chloe wanted to know.

"Four," I said. "We saw four."

"That's enough," Isaac said, "to cause serious damage."

"Will the fire keep them away?"

"For now."

We gripped our sticks tighter, and I kept my eyes on the dark behind the fire, waiting for the eyes to move closer. *It will be okay,* I thought. *As long as they can't get in. They'll have to leave eventually.*

Snuffling. Loud in my ears. A whuffing, then a growl. I jerked up, almost poking my spear into the underside of my chin.

How long have I been asleep? Minutes? Or hours?

I reached my hand out behind me; Oscar was still leaning against my back, his posture and breathing told me he was asleep. "Oscar?"

The snuffling inches away stopped. Silence. I leaned forward, my cheek against the branches. There was a two-inch gap in front of my eyes, and the wolf blinked back at me, gold eyes surrounded by pale fur. Its gaze deepened from surprise to sharp curiosity, and I held my breath, unable to move. Another snort, on the far side of the shelter. A low growl. But the wolf never took its eyes off me.

We were surrounded.

"Oscar?" My voice creaked, my throat constricting to a whisper.

"Hmm?"

"They're here."

"Umm . . ."

I shoved back against him, hard, my eyes never leaving the wolf. He looked big, much bigger this close up, and for some reason I had thought it would be no different from seeing a large dog. But it wasn't like that, not at all. This was no dog. "They're here!" I hissed.

Isaac stirred. "What the . . ."

I leaned forward and shook Chloe's shoulder. I could tell she was awake when I heard her suck her breath in. "Holy—"

"Shhh!" said Oscar. "They're right outside."

"Tell me something I don't know." Isaac shifted himself around in the dark. "But they won't get in."

"How do you know?"

"Because they're wolves, not bears."

"So?"

"Wolves are shy and afraid of people."

"They don't look shy right now," I whispered. "And they certainly don't look afraid." The wolf still had its eyes on me; I wondered what it was thinking.

As I watched, another one (smaller) padded over into my line of sight. I held up my stick, ready to drive it through like a bayonet. What would happen if I did? Would that make it worse? Or would they run? Despite their thick fur, I could see a rangy thinness about them. Were they hungry? As hungry as I was? Maybe all they saw when they looked at us was what we were. Meat.

The wolves growled softly to each other. The smaller one lowered its head and nipped the big one under the chin.

Now we're the meat.

A sharp yelp pierced the silence. "Got ya!" Isaac blurted.

"What are you doing?" Chloe whispered. "Don't make them mad!"

"We need to scare them off!" He huffed. "What do you think? That we're going to just sit in this hut and wait forever."

"Look," Oscar said quietly. "It's almost dawn. They'll probably just leave."

"You don't know that."

I looked out at the fire, which was low but still burning. If no one did anything soon, it would go out in an hour.

"So what should we do?" I asked. "You wanna go out there, Isaac?"

"Actually, I think it's your turn, Dodd."

"I'll pass."

"No one's going out there," Oscar said. "At least not yet. Let's just wait until the sun comes up. I'm sure they'll be gone by then."

"They're wolves, not vampires, Wiener."

"Just trust me."

I couldn't see Isaac's face in the dark, but I could imagine it. I bent my chin and touched it to my knees, desperately wanting to lie down or at least stretch out my arms and legs, but it was too cramped in here with all our gear.

"Just hold on a little longer," Oscar said, sounding much more confident that he should. "And it will be okay."

"Famous last words," replied Isaac, rustling his spear through the cracks.

We went back to watching the wolves as they watched us, waiting for something to happen, and for a long time they circled us. Near dawn the fire turned to cinders, and when I looked up again, jolted awake by the sharp tweet of a cardinal, the wolves were gone, the scattered tracks the only sign of their existence.

Day 8
Morning

"I guess that's it." Oscar double-checked the direction with the watch. "Okay, that's due south."

"East," Isaac said. "We're going east, remember?"

"I know. I was just orienting myself." Oscar turned slightly left while Isaac grunted noncommittally.

We were loaded up, seemingly somewhat heavier than last time, on account of the supply of fish Isaac smoked (fish jerky, he called it), but he warned it probably wouldn't keep past the day. "We need to find another lake or some water," he kept repeating, like a personal mantra. Though we lived with a constant ache of hunger, the main fear was water, namely running out of it. There were hundreds of lakes in the Boundary Waters, but there was also a chance we could hike through miles and miles of woods.

The plan was simple; at least it sounded simple. Hike all day, only stopping at noon to rest. If we hiked at least five miles, Isaac reasoned, and kept on an east heading, at most it would be three days until we had to hit something—another lake, a stream, a campsite, a ranger station, a highway, or best of all, another person with a cell phone.

We headed out, our eyes scanning the trees for movement, and though we didn't talk about last night, I knew everyone was thinking about it. There had been tracks everywhere, some larger than my hand, but Oscar had been right. The wolves had left at dawn. Isaac said they could have just been curious, or they could have been tracking us, and we needed to leave enough time each evening to build a decent shelter. That would slow us down by hours, but it was better than the alternative. And then there was the storm. It could arrive any day now. I glanced nervously through the treetops, but the sky held no clue. Clear deep blue, devoid of clouds.

I concentrated on keeping up with Oscar, who hiked much faster than I did, and I figured as long as we kept this pace, five miles could easily be done by evening.

It didn't take long to see I was overly optimistic.

Soon after we left the lake, a half mile in, we ran into a thicket—a wall of bushes, prickers, burrs, and weeds eight feet high. There was no trail to speak of, so Oscar led the way, holding his pack in front as a shield. I did the same.

"You okay?" I asked Chloe, holding back the branches. Gnats were so thick I had given up trying to spit them out of my mouth. I just chewed and swallowed. Maybe they'd give me some energy. They flew behind my sunglasses in such dense swarms that I had to take them off.

"So far so good." She coughed on the gnats and adjusted her bandana. Oscar had wrapped her foot extra tight before we set out and made her promise to tell him if it started hurting. We would stop, he told us, even if Isaac didn't want to.

"Christ, Wiener!" Isaac yelled from the back of the line. "Where are you taking us?" Isaac was carrying the most weight. His own pack, as well as the fishing gear. He wouldn't let any of us carry it anyway. Apparently he didn't trust us to keep it secure.

"South," Oscar said.

"East!"

"Yeah, that's what I meant," Oscar replied.

"You'd better."

"Just trying to find the easiest way through this."

We pushed through a seemingly endless maze of branches, leaves, and bugs for another hour before we came out the other side. Here were trees, large pines and maples, tall enough to form a solid canopy of shade so that the ground was clear, littered with pine-needle mulch. Ferns grew in clumps in the spaces of dappled sunlight.

"Thank God that's over," I said, wondering at the same time what God had to do with it. I slid off my pack and sat down.

"What are you doing, Dodd?" Isaac demanded. "This ain't a rest stop."

"It is for me."

"We can eat those ramps," Chloe said. When she took off her pack, I knew Isaac was going to be outnumbered.

"What's a ramp?"

"Wild leeks. Like onions."

"What do you mean, like make a salad?" Oscar asked.

"Sure."

Chloe bent down in front of a clump and pulled the bright green stems. I could see she was favoring her foot. Would she tell me if it got bad?

She rummaged around the base of a pine tree, then pulled up two skinny bulbs. They did look like onions. "See? Look."

"You can eat these?" I asked.

"Sure. They serve them in fancy restaurants. Sautéed in butter, of course."

"Of course." Isaac grabbed one, not needing to be told twice. Of all of us, hunger had taken the hardest toll on him, and judging by how much his belt was tightened, he'd lost more than ten pounds. Maybe closer to twenty. He popped it into his mouth and chewed. The watery crunch made my mouth fill with saliva.

"Tastes like onion," he said. "Could use some salt."

"But it's good, right?"

"It's not bad."

In ten minutes we had a pile of ramps to fill a bucket. Then we ate them, along with small sips of water. I tried not to drink more than a fourth of my canteen. It was still morning, and we needed it to last all day. Or whenever we found the next source.

"All right," Oscar said, busy orienting himself again, and I wondered how we would find our way if it suddenly became cloudy. "Let's walk for another hour. I'm sure we'll find water by then."

"You better be taking us the right way," Isaac warned, gulping a swig from his canteen.

"Look!" Oscar yelled back, clearly pissed. "You want to be the navigator?"

"Calm down, Wiener. Quit your bitching! I just want to make sure we're going east."

"I said we were! Now shut up!"

"Come again?"

Oscar spun around. "I said shut up, dickhead!"

"Didn't quite catch that."

"Did I stutter?"

Isaac stared at him, bemused. "Oh, looky here! Looks like you've been hanging around the girls too much. Or maybe taking a page out of Johnson's playbook." He cocked his hip in exaggeration. "Congratulations, Wiener. Now you're a strong, confident black woman who doesn't take shit from whitey. Yes, suh! You go, girl!" He snapped his fingers derisively.

Chloe gasped. I couldn't tell by her face whether she was surprised or not.

I wasn't. "You stupid pig!"

"A pig, huh?" Isaac turned his attention to me. "And what are *you*, Dodd?" He jabbed a finger at me like he wanted to poke me in the eye. "I'm the one who saved your asses, remember? I caught the food! I pulled you dumb fucks up the side of the cliff!"

"Yeah!" Chloe screamed. "After you abandoned us!"

"It's not my fault you're too damn slow to keep up!"

"I got hurt!"

"That's not my fault either!" Isaac's eyes narrowed to dangerous slits. "You bunch of idiots would all be dead right now if it weren't for me."

"We made the shelter, remember?" Chloe yelled, finding her stride. "We made the raft!"

"*That* was a stupid idea!"

I shouldn't have been surprised; I knew that's what he thought, but it just took him until now to say it. "You're a gigantic asshole!"

"And you!" he roared. "You're a stuck-up little bitch, aren't you? You think you're better than me?" He dropped his tackle box and leaped in front me, his face disfigured with rage. "I should've screwed you when I had the chance."

All the blood drained from my face; I couldn't have been more speechless if he'd punched me.

Oscar gasped. "What did you say?"

"You heard me," he said with an oily smile. "She likes to play hard to get, doesn't she? Did she take off her clothes for you, too?"

Oscar's face looked like he'd been given a series of strong electric shocks.

"Get away from me!" I pushed him forward, slapping his hands away. "Drop dead, you piece of shit!"

"Ladies, first." Isaac began to bow but suddenly went sideways in a blur of movement.

Oscar hit him square in the chest, and they collapsed into a heap, tumbling over each other on the ground, packs clanking together as they punched and cursed and kicked, then rolled away and disappeared into a mass of ferns. The last thing I saw was Oscar, jabbing a swift punch underneath Isaac's chin.

"Stop it!" Chloe screeched. She jumped up to follow but winced and sank back down. "Emma! Stop them!"

I stood rooted to the ground in my boots, mouth open and wondering if I had just imagined the whole thing, but the bushes were still shaking from the force of impact, and a few moments later there was another crashing noise, now some distance away.

"Emma!" Chloe yanked my arm. "Stop them before they kill each other!"

What she didn't say: *Stop it before Isaac kills Oscar.*

I ran forward into the ferns, blood roaring in my ears. Isaac wouldn't do that, would he? He was bigger than Oscar. Then again, Oscar was furious. Then again, Isaac was crazy. Who would win in a fight like that? Furious versus insane.

Insane. That is the only winner in this kind of game.

I pushed my way through the thicket, not even feeling the prickers scratch my hands. *Where did they go?* I took a few more steps and stopped, listening. Heavy breathing, then another grunt. A thudding smack, the distinctive sound of a fist making contact. Then screaming. Or more specifically, one distinct scream.

Oscar!

The trees pressed together in thick clumps, then thinned out, and I pushed forward through the undergrowth, leaves and branches whipping at my chin. *Where did they go? How can they have just disappeared so fast?*

"Oscar!"

No answer, just a woodpecker, drilling the side of a cedar. I counted to five.

"Jesus Christ! Dammit!" Isaac. And he sounded close.

I turned around. "Where are you?"

"Here! Help!"

In front of me. Dead ahead. *They are so close. Why can't I see them?* I jumped through the bush, but my pack yanked me backward, something caught in a nylon loop. I jerked it, but it was stuck, so I slipped my arms out, then stumbled forward on a landslide of pebbles, and my feet went out from under me. I landed on my butt, slid through the branches until a cold gust of wind hit my face as my feet shot out into open air. *What the—*

I had almost slid right off the side of a cliff.

"Jesus!" I scrambled back, my hands instinctively reaching

for something, anything, to grab on to while I kicked more pebbles and sand off the side. *If I hadn't fallen down, I would have gone right off the edge.*

"Ow! Stop it, dammit!"

"Oscar?" Oh my God, they fell off the side! I swallowed in horror, but something stayed lodged in my throat. I inched forward on my stomach, my head spinning at the idea.

"Here!"

I peered over the side, terrified of what I was going to see.

Isaac's dirt-streaked face stared back, three feet below me, one fist clenched around a very fragile-looking protrusion of rock, the other holding tightly to the shoulder strap of Oscar's backpack. Oscar, thankfully, was still in it. And below them, at least sixty feet away, was the ground.

Oh God oh God oh God oh God. I shuddered back, dizzy and sick, my vision swirling dangerously.

"Emma!" Isaac gasped. "Help me!"

He actually used my first name! Shit! Think!

"Just hang on!" How could I help? I wasn't strong enough to pull them up. "Chloe!" I screamed. I needed my pack. I needed a rope. I needed a plan. Fast.

"Hurry!" Isaac panted. "I can't hold him forever!"

Him. Oh no. Oscar!

"You better, goddamn it!" I forced myself to look back over the edge. Oscar had absolutely nothing to hold on to, and if Isaac let go . . . I blinked away the thought. "I'll fucking kill you myself if you drop him!"

Still shaking, I crawled back through the bushes on my hands and knees, my head buzzing from the sight of them clinging to the rocks like flies. *What am I going to do?*

"Emma?" Chloe's boots were suddenly in front of my face. "What are you—"

"Stop!" I screamed, throwing my hands up. "Just stop! A cliff!"

"Huh?"

I pushed myself onto my knees, blocking her. "You can't see it!" I glanced back; the edge was only a few feet behind me but completely masked by a screen of leaves.

"Where are . . ."

"Hanging on the side!" I held my hand up, trying to think of what to do. "We need a rope! Something to pull them up." I jumped to my feet. "Now!"

Chloe just nodded, eyes wide, and dropped her pack with no more questions. She unzipped it and removed the contents in handfuls. I loved her then. "Clothes! Clothes will work."

"Clothes?"

"We can tie them together and make a rope." She pulled out an electric-blue bra and tugged at the elastic strap. "Can you make a strong knot?"

"I don't know!" I wanted to keep screaming; I felt like an idiot, petrified by panic, but Chloe was already busy with a pair of ripstop nylon pants and a long-sleeved T-shirt.

"How long does it have to be?"

"Ten feet? Longer? And we need to secure it to something."

"Here!" She tossed me a shirt. "Do a square knot to tie to the pants."

I stretched the sleeves apart, wondering what to do next. "Uh . . ."

"Never mind, I got it." She already had her wad of clothes knotted together. "I'll anchor this around the tree like a noose." She slipped the bra around the aspen, looping the strap three times, pulling the long part through. "Okay, good." She tossed me more clothes. "Stretchy stuff is better."

I grabbed another long-sleeved shirt, a thin polyester hoodie, a sports bra, and a swimsuit, mimicking the knots I'd seen her make. I tugged hard; they held. But would they hold with more than two hundred pounds?

I crawled back through the bushes to the edge, unraveling the line, checking each knot.

"I have it secured!" Chloe yelled.

"Okay!" I dangled the line over the side, down past Isaac's face, which was pressed tightly against the cliff. "Grab this!"

"No." His voice sounded wispy and raw. "If I grab it, I'll drop Wiener. Slide it down to him first."

Either he was trying to be a hero, or he didn't trust my rope, but I wasn't about to argue. I snaked the line down farther, until it hit against Oscar's shoulder. "Grab it!" Isaac ordered. "Because I'm about five seconds from dropping you!"

Dear God, please hold.

The line tightened in my grip. Immediately I was overcome

with the urge to pull back, brace myself, dig in my heels, do something, anything other than sit there to watch what might happen. I clenched my eyes shut and held on, counting seconds, waiting for a screaming free fall.

But soon enough Oscar's face appeared in front of me, bruised and scraped, missing his glasses. I'd never been happier to see it. "Emma." He crawled forward and collapsed into a shaking heap on my lap, clenching his left arm tight to his chest. "I think I broke my wrist."

I was shaking too. "It's okay, it's okay," I babbled, not able to tell whether I was going to laugh or cry. Maybe pass out. "We can fix that." I ran my fingers through his hair and squeezed. "We can fix that."

Isaac pulled his way up, grunting with effort, and crawled past us, a glazed look etched on his face. He rolled onto his back and stared blindly at the sky, gripping the clothes rope to his chest like it was a baby blanket, and after a long while he finally spoke, his voice muted in amazement. "A bra just saved my life."

We hiked on until the shadows lengthened to thin strips. Isaac guessed we'd gone five or six miles, maybe seven, but we also hadn't found any water. When we found a small clearing in the trees, we decided to stop and make camp. Chloe constructed a makeshift hut woven together with flexible dogwood branches, and while it was enough to block the wind, it wasn't nearly as solid as our previous shelter.

It didn't think it would stop the wolves if they returned.

I went back to finishing my spears. Four done, but would that be enough? I grabbed another stick and stripped a thin slice of bark off the tip.

"Want some help, Dodd?" Isaac actually sounded sincere, maybe his way of apologizing. Or maybe his way of thanking me and Chloe for saving his life. Whatever it was, he certainly couldn't call us useless idiots. Idiots maybe. But definitely not useless.

"I'm almost done." I didn't know how to talk to him, or look at him. Every time I did, I saw his face, twisted in simmering violence. All along, I had thought the danger we were in was the outside: storms, fire, thirst, hunger, animals. But what was worse when it came down to it? Being hungry or depending on a psychopath for survival? But was he really? He sounded a bit guilty, or maybe that was fake too, just another attempt to manipulate me. There was no way for me to trust him.

"Okay." Isaac picked up a spear and poked it against his palm. "Wiener thinks his wrist is broken."

"Yeah, probably." I tossed the stick into the pile, wondering why he cared. "Or at least sprained badly. Chloe wrapped it and made a sling with the Ace bandage." I glanced over at Oscar, who was sleeping (maybe) in the new shelter. He didn't act like he was in a lot of pain, but then again I had heard him gasp several times when Chloe was wrapping his wrist. It had to hurt like hell, even if it wasn't broken.

"But now she doesn't have anything for her ankle." He sounded confused, as if he couldn't understand how someone would make a choice like that.

"I guess we'll improvise." I pointed my knife at a cut-up piece of elastic fabric. "Women's lingerie can save your life, remember?" I didn't mention the fact that it was us (two girls) who actually did. But as it turned out, I didn't need to.

"Thanks," Isaac said, low, and I knew this was as much as I was going to get. Strangely, it was enough.

I nodded, picked up another stick to whittle, not looking up until I heard him leave. A growing part of me understood that I wouldn't have saved his life. Not if he'd been alone. I did it because of Oscar. I would have watched Isaac fall; I was certain. Watched him fall and done nothing. Maybe I would have even pushed him. I bit my lip, so hot and flustered with the sudden knowledge that I had to stop whittling. I closed the blade and pressed the knife between my hands until they ached.

But the reality was Isaac hadn't let Oscar fall. Despite everything, he'd held on. So what, in the end, did that make him? Not a coward, but maybe not a hero, either. And I guess not a total psychopath. He was someone who would succeed where others would fail. He actually could save someone's life.

Something I had failed to do.

So what does that make me?

Day 9
Morning

"Morning, sunshine."

I scraped at my tongue with my toothbrush and grunted back. *He's still acting like nothing's wrong. Like he did nothing wrong. Unbelievable.*

"I guess you're not a morning person, huh?" Isaac was eating one of the little brick food packets from Chloe's e-kit. I had eaten mine yesterday, as soon as Chloe handed me the packet, and it was hard to believe that Isaac had had enough restraint to wait until this morning. I could smell the peanut butter from here, and I wondered how much food he had left. *Probably nothing.*

I pulled out my toothbrush and spat. "I'm a morning person as long as coffee is involved."

"I prefer Mountain Dew. But this isn't bad."

"I could go for a donut right now. Chocolate."

"Ah, donuts." Isaac crumpled his wrapper—the sound

made me drool a bit. What did I have left to eat? My packets of oatmeal. A toy-size box of cereal. *No, wait. I ate the cereal two days ago.* Maybe *I* should start looking for food. What grew out here besides berries and mushrooms?

A mosquito hummed in my ear. Barely morning but they were having their breakfast. Me.

"Do you think they'll come today?" I don't know why I asked—maybe just for something to say. I didn't think they were coming today. Whoever *they* were. Firefighters? Rangers? Police? Volunteers?

"Nope." Isaac dug a hole in the dirt, stuck in the wrapper, and buried it, smoothing the ground into a gravelike mound.

"Maybe a plane tomorrow."

"Doubt it."

"Well, when then, you think? Three days? Five?"

Isaac glared at the trees. "How about never."

"Why?"

He stood up and crossed his arms. He was combative as usual, but there was something else. His eyes glittered wet. "Because, Dodd. They're not coming."

"I don't believe you." But a growing part of me did, every single word. *They think we're dead. They think we died in the fire. They looked. They found the campsite.*

"Doesn't matter if you believe me or not. The sooner you realize you're on your own, the better off you'll be."

"But we're not on our own," I argued. "They're looking for us. They haven't given up on us. There's been a plane." My mind leaped to my parents. What would they do? What could they do? Were they out there, looking for me? Would they give up? And how do you do that, even? How does a person let go? How does a person lose all their children? It would be like losing your future. Every dream and every wish you ever had. It was losing hope. How could you stand that? How could anyone?

But Isaac was already packing up his stuff. "Take it from one who knows, Dodd. They *can* give up on us. They already have." He zipped his pack shut and glanced up through the treetops. Another blue-sky morning, but I did the math in my head. Chris said the storm was coming in—what? A week. And today was day nine, which meant . . . *shit.* The storm could hit at any moment. It was always there, in the back of our minds, running down like a doomsday clock. "Better wake them up, because we're leaving in five minutes. And it's gonna be a long walk."

"How much longer?"

"Ten klicks."

"Come again?"

Isaac sighed. "We still got a ways."

"Ten klicks is ten kilometers," I said, leaning up against a sapling without trying to look like I was. I had no intention of letting him think I was exhausted. "Ten kilometers is over six miles," I added, trying not to sound like a total smart-ass.

I failed. Isaac smirked at me in delight. "Maybe you should join the army, Dodd."

I uncapped my canteen and took a swig. "We need to get out of here first, I think."

Isaac glanced back to the wispy trail we had made, waiting for Chloe and Oscar. "Which is why we need to keep going." He tapped his own (empty) canteen against his fist. "The storm, remember? We'll be in deep shit if it turns into a blizzard up here."

I desperately wanted to drain the last quarter of my canteen but somehow restrained myself. My tongue felt twice as thick as normal, and it hurt to swallow. "At least we'll have something to drink then."

"We'll freeze to death first." Isaac wiped the sweat from his forehead; he was wearing a thin T-shirt, and the backs of his arms were speckled with bright pink dots.

"That doesn't look good." I pointed at them, and upon closer inspection they looked more like welts than mosquito bites. "You should probably use more bug spray."

He dropped his arms, eyes suddenly wide. "What?"

"Bug bites," I said slowly, realizing that I had seen that type of mark before. Even before I finished speaking, I knew they weren't bug bites. They looked like burn marks from a cigarette. My friend Shelly had burned herself once with a lit cigarette, laughing because she was drunk. And it had left a similar scar. And they were on the backs of his arm, in such a position that I knew he hadn't put them there himself.

Someone else had. My throat seemed to swell shut with this knowledge, and I had to turn my face away.

"Right, okay." Isaac zipped open his pack and busied himself with finding a can.

The crack of pine needles behind me let me know Chloe and Oscar had caught up. Oscar walked through the small hole in the brush, then held the branches back for Chloe, who was moving very slowly, stepping somewhat gingerly on her bad foot. And although her limp was barely noticeable, I knew if she overdid it, we'd be right back where we started. But this time, I highly doubted Oscar would be able to carry her.

"How you doing?" I asked.

"Okay." Chloe smiled weakly. "Just thirsty."

Oscar shrugged, looking past me without answering. The whole morning had been like that, and I wasn't very good at tolerating the silent treatment. I knew he was pissed, at Isaac mainly, but also at me, and I knew I should tell him what Isaac had done. What he really had done.

But then what would happen? I couldn't take the risk of another fight between them, but I also knew I had to fix it. Somehow. "We'll go until we find some water," I said, ignoring the look Isaac gave me. "And then we'll rest." I adjusted my pack, tightening up the strap against my stomach, hoping the pressure would dull the ache inside.

"Lead on, Kemosabe," Isaac said. "Since, unlike some of us, you're not so directionally challenged."

I couldn't tell if that was an insult or a compliment but figured the best thing to do was ignore it completely. *Just walk*, I thought. *Just keep moving. If we keep going, eventually we'll hit something; eventually we'll find Lake Superior. We have to.*

Day 9
Evening

We walked for what seemed like hours in silence. No planes. No helicopters. No chain saws. Only the sound of shrieking birds in the trees and, finally, the soothing trickle of a shallow creek, something we had stumbled on (literally) when Chloe spied a dark ravine from a hilly rise. We scrambled down the hill quick as we dared, found a narrow animal trail through the trees, which led to a pebbly creek bed that fed into a tiny pond. The pond itself was scuzzy, coated with algae and weedy plants, but it was water, and it was where we would camp for the night.

Since there was no food left (and nothing found on the hike), that meant a meal of oatmeal. *The Last Supper*. We combined all our packets into the pot with boiling water, then added more water to thin it out to a souplike consistency. Banana-strawberry-blueberry-peach gruel. Oscar found a stick the exact size and shape of a wooden spoon, and we almost burned our mouths because it tasted so good.

But it didn't go far. It was just the right amount of food to make us want more. A lot more, but there was nothing left. Completely gone. I still felt okay (despite a near-constant headache), but my stomach had definitely shrunk. My skin seemed looser, like a partially deflated balloon. If I pinched the skin on my hand, it didn't snap and flatten back immediately. It stayed in a white crease, like an old person. Or maybe that was a sign of dehydration. Probably both. But still, I wasn't suffering as much as everyone else. Isaac looked like he'd shrunk a few inches, and both Chloe and Oscar had shaded hollows under their eyes. Then again, I hadn't looked in a mirror in a week. Maybe I looked worse.

When we finished taking turns scraping the bottom of the pot, we sat quietly, listening to the fire.

"So, no fish in that pond, huh?" Chloe's question was innocent enough, but it could only be interpreted as an accusation.

Isaac scraped a bit of oatmeal from the pot and set it down. "Nope."

"How about the snares?"

"Nothing."

"Well, maybe tomorrow." Chloe poked her stick in the fire, trying to sound optimistic.

"Yeah," Isaac said darkly. "Maybe tomorrow."

A depression like smoke descended around us.

"Do we need more bait?" I asked.

"Are you volunteering, Dodd?"

"I guess," I said. "Yes. I'm volunteering."

"Well, good luck with that. I found three night crawlers, a fat grub, and some ugly beetle," he said. "And I only caught a box turtle, but it slipped off the hook before I could reel him in." He sniffed and rolled his eyes, as if daring me to do better.

"Oh." I stubbed my stick at the fire, careful to keep my eyes down, knowing all through the course of dinner I had become increasingly aware of Oscar's glances. His hand held the stick-spoon longer when he passed it to me. His eyes kept landing on mine, full of only one question. He even sat closer, angling himself toward me. I did nothing.

The fire climbed and fell, and finally I yawned and excused myself. There was nothing more to eat, so I grabbed the empty cook pot.

"Where you going?" Chloe asked.

"To wash it. The oatmeal will stick on like cement." I glanced down—the pot was spotless, not an oat left. "Well, usually it sticks. I guess I'll go rinse it out and get more water."

I was halfway down the trail when I heard Oscar say, "I'm going to bed."

"Sweet dreams," Isaac called back.

I crouched down at the water's edge and submerged the pot, swirling it clean before I refilled it.

Footsteps behind me, crunching on pebbles, turned my head.

"Hey." Oscar sat down, but this time he looked directly

at me, obviously waiting for me to say something. Or maybe do something. His gaze was unnerving. He wanted an explanation.

"Hey." I filled the pot to the brim.

It was quiet, but not really, not when I really stopped to listen. Peeping frogs, twittering birds, leaves rustling in the wind, and below all that the constant hum of insects. Even with all the sounds I could still hear Isaac and Chloe talking. Their words were unintelligible, but it sounded more like a conversation, less like a brewing fight. I cocked my head in their direction. "That's a first."

"Wonder how long it will last."

"Five minutes, maybe."

"Wonder what they're talking about."

"I don't know." I made a face at the water, the flash of Isaac pressing me up against the tree made me drop the pot. Just like that he had changed, as unpredictable as a wild animal, maybe even more so. And I had never seen it coming. "I don't know anything." I kept filling and emptying the pot of water.

"You know how to survive," he said. "That's something."

"That's just dumb luck."

"I don't think so."

I started up to go back to the campfire. Oscar didn't follow me. I didn't expect him to. But when I passed, he grabbed my elbow, pulling back gently, like he was directing a kite on a string, and I couldn't help but notice how different his touch felt on my skin than Isaac's. "Don't go." I looked down at the top of his head, but he was only watching the creek. "Not now. Don't go."

I didn't want to go. "They want the water." It was a stupid protest.

"They can wait." His voice was thick, heavy with something. His grip tightened.

I sank down and dropped the pot, letting the water run in rivulets back to the source. *Does it matter anymore what we do? Does anything matter?*

"Maybe," Oscar answered, and I knew I had been thinking out loud again. "I think some things do matter."

"What Isaac said before," I began, feeling shaky and embarrassed. "He saw me get out of the water when I took a bath. He wouldn't give me my towel." I swallowed with some difficulty, thinking about what to say next. No way was I going to tell him what had happened in the woods. Not now. Not ever. I couldn't risk another fight. "That's it. That's all. He made it sound like something different."

"Oh." I could see the lines of veins pulse in his throat.

"He's an asshole."

Oscar turned to me with a quiet smile. "Oh really? I hadn't noticed." Without his glasses on, his eyes looked even darker, more black than brown. He exhaled slow and heavy; I could see his whole frame relax, tension sinking away.

"I just wanted to explain."

"You don't have to explain yourself to me, Emma."

"I want to."

"I believe you, you know," Oscar said. "It's okay."

"Good." I exhaled. "Just don't get into any more fights, okay? It's not worth it. It doesn't matter what Isaac says."

"It matters to me." His voice was hard, remembering.

"But we need to stick together or we won't make it. We need to get along." It was a simple statement. An opinion. A fact. An undeniable truth. I shook my head. "We'll all die out here."

"All the more reason then." He pulled me to him, his mouth quieting mine, and that was good, because there really was nothing left to say. He was right. All the more reason.

We attacked each other like we were starving. Because we actually were. His fingers wound through my hair, and I gripped the back of his head, our noses and teeth clicking together when our lips collided. He tasted like dirt and sand and leaves, salty and sweet water, and it made me even hungrier. I rolled back down onto my shoulders, conscious of his wrist, and that one small gesture was all the invitation he needed. He slid his good arm underneath the small of my back, following me down with a soft sigh. My lips were numb, almost bruised, but his tongue was warm in my mouth, each kiss sending small electrical shocks through my veins until I was certain my blood was boiling. The roar of it echoed in my head, but all I could think was more. I wanted more. I needed more. I panted like I'd sprinted a mile but knew I could keep going. I definitely wanted to keep going. I bit his lip gently, moved my hands down his chest, pressing myself closer. Oscar responded by running his hand up the inside of my thigh and cupping his palm firmly against me. I felt like I might go blind from the sensation. Seeing my reaction, Oscar proceeded to unbutton my shirt.

"Hey, Dodd? Where's the water?" Isaac yelled. "Are you doing a rain dance down there?"

Oscar pulled back and looked down at me, his eyes a blur of anxiety and lust and bewilderment. I must have looked the same, because he immediately sat up and apologized.

"I'm sorry." He cradled his bad wrist against his chest, wincing.

"For what?" I sat up and picked a leaf out of my hair.

He exhaled a bit shakily, his mouth quivering with the words. "I don't know."

"You don't have to be sorry," I said, realizing it sounded exactly like something my psychiatrist would say. I decided to finish the line. "You didn't do anything wrong."

"Says you."

"Yeah, says me." I couldn't figure out why his mood had changed so abruptly. Then again, I often did the same thing. He almost seemed scared, not of me exactly, but of himself. I shook my head, letting the dirt sift out. That was just my crazy talking again.

His fear made me brave, if only to reassure him. "You don't

have to do anything you don't want to do." *There, my therapist training is complete.*

He swiveled around to face me and swallowed hard. "That's just it," he said. "I do want to. I want to so badly I can't even think of anything else."

Flattery was warm syrup in my blood, flushing me with pleasure. "And that's so bad?"

"Out here it is." He nodded, serious. "Out here it can get us killed."

"It can get you killed anywhere."

"More here, I think."

I sighed and stood up (still tingling). "We'll see." I refilled the pot of water and walked back to the fire.

Day 10
Morning

We're going to die. I scratched the sentence into the dirt with a stick, read it to myself several times, then stepped on it, smearing the words with my boot. I refilled the pot and grabbed my fresh stack of kindling.

I settled the cook pot on the ring of rocks (a makeshift stovetop) and watched it until bubbles pricked up from the bottom.

"What's on the itinerary today, Dodd?" Isaac cut a fat worm into thirds, using a sharp rock. He smiled at me, obviously looking for dirt. I had no idea why he thought I would tell him anything, but it's not like I could blame him. No TV. No Internet. No cards, no music, and the only other object of entertainment we had possessed we used to start a fire.

"We need to find some food before we leave."

"No shit we do. What do you think you're gonna find?"

"Mushrooms. Berries. I don't know."

"Wiener going with you?"

"No."

"Really? Why not?" His grin was pure evil.

"I think he went to find more wood for the fire."

Immediately I regretted my choice of words. *Three, two, one . . .*

"More wood? I know what wood he'd like to give ya."

"You're such a delicate flower, aren't you?"

"I try." He stuck the hook through a chunk of worm, wrapping it around into a juicy knot, running it through the barb twice, making it impossible for a fish to remove. "Maybe I should go with you."

Hell no. "I think you should stick to fishing." I picked up the empty oatmeal box, all thoughts turned to food. Even that worm was starting to look good.

"Take the shirt strips if you're going," he commanded. "Take the whistle and don't go far. We still need to do five miles today."

Since when do you care, you creep? "Check and check." I tugged at the whistle around my neck.

"Well, well." Isaac smiled.

"Well, well, what? What does that mean?"

"Didn't know girls could plan ahead."

"Since when?"

His blue eyes were brittle in the morning light. "My old man used to say that women couldn't be soldiers. Said they were too sensitive. Said they were too emotional. Would panic when the shit hit the fan."

"Oh really?"

"Also said they would bleed five days a month and what do you do with someone like that?"

"What's your point?" I crossed my arms, waiting.

"My point?" Isaac looked at me as though I was an idiot. "My point is that my old man didn't want those bitches in combat. Thought they couldn't do the job as well as a man."

"That's not a point," I said. "That's an opinion. My opinion is that your dad sounds like an asshole."

"Actually, that's a fact." Isaac smiled, as though I got the joke. "My dad *is* an asshole."

I walked off clutching the box to my chest. "I don't give two shits what your dad thinks." *Or you.*

Mushrooms grew in shade. In damp places. On rotted, moss-covered logs.

I didn't know where to start. Everything looked shady and damp, so I just started walking, edging the pond with my eyes on the ground, looking for creamy white buttons in all the brown and green. After a while, I realized looking at the ground might be a good way to get lost, so I made sure to keep the water on my left side, staying close enough to always see it through the trees.

My stomach burned as I walked, and I prayed Isaac would catch something. After I walked for thirty minutes or so, I came to a place where the trees thinned out. Against the blue sky I couldn't see the trail of smoke from the campfire, which depressed me. I wasn't that far. How could I expect a plane to see it? I walked a few more yards and sat down to rest. The breeze was stronger today. Fewer bugs. That was a plus. I was too tired. Lack of food will do that, I guess. I didn't know how long I sat there until a flash of movement caught the corner of my eye. Animal movement, darting and weaving through the trees. I froze, not even daring to turn my head. *What is it? What is it?* Small, sleek, orange and black, splotches of gray and white. Oh my God. I shoved my hand in my pocket and pulled out my knife, flicking up the blade with trembling fingers. When I glanced up again, it was in front of me, five yards away, blinking curiously with bright gold eyes.

A fox. And not just a fox. It carried a dead rabbit in its mouth.

All I saw was breakfast.

I jumped up, clutching my empty oatmeal box and canteen. "Gimme that," I told the fox, which blinked and wheeled in the other direction, breaking into a lazy trot. I followed, sprinting quickly, my eyes on its tail. It wasn't moving fast, and it clearly wasn't afraid of me, but there was no way I was quick enough to catch up with it. What would happen if I did? The fox turned its head back, then darted sideways underneath a bush. *Just drop it,* I thought. If I got close enough, maybe it would get scared and abandon it. I pushed through the thicket in time for a glimpse of a white tail vanishing behind a rock. I took two giant steps before something caught my foot. I went down like a felled tree, and though normally I would have had the presence of mind to put my hands out, in the process of jumping up and running (on an empty stomach), all the blood from my brain had drained down as though a plug had been pulled from the base of my head. Splinters of light punctured the view in front of me, which was the image of a large rock, growing larger as it rushed up to my face. I didn't even have time to wonder what was going to happen next, let alone put my hands up.

Everything went black.

Rose-red light flickered behind my eyelids, and when I opened them, wispy clouds threaded through the solid blue sky above me. I pushed myself up slowly. My forehead throbbed in time with my pulse, and my fingers came away red and sticky when I touched the sore spot. I fumbled for my canteen. It was half empty, and I quickly drank the rest.

What happened?

I was looking for something. Mushrooms.

The fox. The rabbit.

I scrambled up, but everything went hazy, slanting side-ways, so I exhaled slowly through my nose and sat back down. I needed to go slow, do everything slow. *What happened to my shirt markers?* I looked down; they were still tied to my pack. *How long have I been here?*

Panic started like a virus, making me sweat. I didn't have any idea how long I'd been unconscious, but the sun was already past the high point in the sky, so I'd been away for a few hours, at least. And no one found me. *Did they even look?*

I staggered up, moving headlong through the trees in determination. Even though it was afternoon, it was gloomy in the shade, and I kept tripping over the uneven terrain. Wet, spongy ground under my boots made sucking sounds when I walked. *Is this the way I came from? This doesn't look familiar at all.* I needed to go back, but which way was it? All the trees looked the same, flinging violet shadows on the ground, stretching out around me. They looked different here—thinner, stragglier.

A pale glow at the base of a dark trunk grabbed my attention. When I got closer, I saw the base of the tree studded with them. Mushrooms. Before, I had never liked them, but I was so hungry, my stomach so pinched and hot, that I almost cried at the sight. I crouched down; I knew I had to be careful, and I picked one and held it up. Was it a morel? An oyster? A button? A puffball? *Or was it something dangerous, like a toadstool?* I closed my eyes, trying to remember the pictures I'd seen in the field guide. Toadstools were poisonous. What were the others? Destroying angel. Death cap. Ivory funnel. This kind looked like a morel, light tan with a pointed spongy honeycomb top, reminding me of a tiny brain. It smelled like wood and dirt, and something slightly meaty that made me drool. *Do I?* I shouldn't, I knew that, but I was so hungry that a second later I rubbed it on my tongue. No real taste to it. Bland. I popped it in my mouth and chewed. Firm. Chewy. Not bad. I swallowed it and grabbed another. *Just one or two more.* Before long I had eaten them all. But I was still hungry. Maybe there would be more on the next tree. I could harvest them and bring a bunch back.

I took another step forward and my right foot sank, cold water bolting up my leg like an electrical shock. What? It was supposed to be trees and grass, but the ground gave way, revealing dark water. Was I going to sink? A loud burp in front of me almost made me pee my pants. Then again, I was too dehydrated.

I blinked repeatedly, but the fat frog in front of me didn't disappear. His bulbous eyes stared back, dull and unafraid. Had he ever seen a person before? He hopped toward me, and the ground quivered where he landed.

Quicksand? No. Ridiculous. There is no sand here. The air vibrated with insects. Dragonflies flitted in iridescent flashes around me.

The frog hopped again, now within my reach. Could I? Should I? I still had my box, but it was my stomach that decided for me. *I'm gonna eat you.* I stayed still—one leg in what I now realized was a bog. I read once that bogs had no end, no base, not like a lake or a river with a measureable depth. There were just layers and layers that became a bottomless pit.

A chorus of burps echoed. More frogs, all singing in the

swamp. The one near me was as large as my hand, and as he hopped forward once more, I bent down and scooped him up. He didn't struggle, and before I even gave it another thought, I took him in one hand by the hind legs and snapped him like a whip, cracking his head against the log. I did it twice, then checked for any jerking. The frog was still. I put him in the oatmeal box.

When I left a few minutes later, mainly because the box was full with eight big ones, I was speckled with mosquito bites. I turned in the opposite direction of the sun and walked until I found the edge of the ravine, my boots squishing out a rhythm that I hummed a rhyme to. *I like frogs, on the logs, I find in bogs.* A blister sprouted on my heel, and by the time I reached the campsite, it had swelled into a painful, fluid-filled cushion, ripe for popping.

"Holy shit on a stick!" Isaac blurted as I strode into the campsite. "What happened to you?"

I touched my forehead again; a nice lump had developed, but the blood must have dried, because it shed crusty red flakes on my fingers.

"Saying you look like a hobo would be a compliment." Isaac went back to baiting more hooks with worms. Apparently, he hadn't caught anything. "Wiener's been looking for you all damn morning," he continued. "He looked like he was one step away from taking a ride to crazy town." The thought made him smile. "I told him to settle down and said, 'Dodd can take care of herself.' Am I right?"

I nodded, my throat a hard, gnarly knot that kept me silent.

"Yeah, well, I thought Wiener was gonna knock my teeth out."

I set the box down just as Chloe and Oscar came around the corner. Even at this distance I could see their relief.

"Oh, Emma!" Chloe said. "Where have you been?"

Oscar didn't say anything, his face impenetrable. He turned away with a quick gasp, and his shoulders heaved twice. He bent over and wiped his eyes, as if there were dust in them.

"I'm okay," I croaked, massaging the knot out of my throat with shaky fingers. "I was out looking for food. I fell. I think I fainted or something." I didn't want to tell them about the fox and the rabbit; I didn't want them to know how close I'd come only to fail.

"You fainted?" Chloe was worried. "Are you sure you're okay? We've been calling and looking for hours. And you took the whistle."

"Sorry," I mumbled, embarrassed. "I must have low blood sugar."

"Well, thank God." She swallowed nervously, then hugged me so hard my back cracked. "I'm just glad you're okay."

"Me too. No big deal," I said. "I was just looking for mushrooms and blueberries."

"Did you find any?" Oscar finally spoke, sounding breathless.

"No," I lied. I hadn't found more, and I didn't want to tell them I'd eaten all the mushrooms like a greedy pig. "I did find something though." I nudged the oatmeal box with my toe.

Chloe peered in. "What the?" She straightened back up, appalled. "Frogs?"

"Frogs?" Isaac perked up. "How many?"

"Eight," I said, proud.

Oscar lifted one from the box, palming it in his hand. It was as round as a baseball. "I think the French call them *grenouilles*. I guess they taste like chicken."

"Well, I call them lunch." Isaac grabbed the box. "Surf or turf, I don't care."

Chloe hesitated. "I don't know if I can eat a frog."

"More for me then." Isaac was already busy using a sharpened stick to remove the guts, and when he was done with that, he skewered them in one long row.

Chloe did end up eating the frog. Actually, she ate two. We all did, nearly burning our mouths waiting for the crackling flesh to cool. And we licked our fingers after.

They tasted better than chicken.

Oscar's eyes followed me the rest of the afternoon. Warm brown eyes, attentive, questioning, patient, and eager at the same time. They were the kind of eyes you didn't want to disappoint.

So I stayed close to the campfire, sharpening the blade on my knife. "Where's Chloe?"

"Learning to fish," I think.

"Really?" I couldn't imagine spending any free time with

Isaac. "I hope she catches something. A whole wad would be nice."

Oscar laughed. "A wad?"

"Or is it called a mess."

"A pod maybe?"

"That's dolphins."

"How about a murder."

"That's crows." It became a game, to see who knew the most.

"A herd."

"A pride."

"A flock."

"A parliament."

"Parliament?" Oscar stared at me. "You made that up."

"No, I didn't."

"What animal is that, then?"

"Owls."

"Serious?"

"Uh-huh." I dragged the blade of the knife at a forty-five-degree angle against a piece of rock, pulling it up sharply. I liked the sound it made, and after a few strokes I held it up to the light to check my work. The steel looked brighter, at least. I pushed it against my palm—definitely sharper. "Here." I handed it to him. "This should work better now. In case we need to gut any more frogs."

"Thanks." He held my hand a few seconds longer than necessary.

"No problem." He kept holding it. Was he going to pull me forward? Kiss me again? I couldn't tell by the look on his face, undecided. I wanted him to decide.

"I mean it," he said, low. "Thank you."

"For what?"

"For you. For them." He titled his head back and examined another cloudless blue sky. "For not being out here alone."

I thought about that. He was right—we wouldn't stand a chance out here by ourselves. Not for this long, anyway. I needed him. We needed each other. I squeezed the slim knife against his grip. "Me too," I said, meaning it. I was alive. I was here. And for the first time in over a year I wanted to keep it that way.

Day 10
Night

My head spun. Waves of heat crashed against my face, then bursts of cold. My neck and chest dripped with sweat, and I struggled to push the covers off. The ceiling pressed down, suffocating me. *No. Not again. I can't do this again.*

I bolted upright, making blood pound painfully behind my eyes, and for a moment I was blind. I heard the creek—wet lapping noises like a thirsty dog slopping water out of a bowl. I was thirsty. So thirsty. My throat burned. Something buzzed near my ear, an electric static hum. I needed something. Something. I had to get out of here. Where was I? I crawled forward, feeling with my hands, inching forward on my knees. A cold breeze hit the back of my neck. It was dark out here. Too dark. I pressed my face down. The dirt was cold, so nice and cold against my skin. In comparison I was so sticky, my clothes clinging to my body in sweaty wads of fabric. But my mouth was bone dry. The nausea came back, and I rolled over, pressing my fist into the pit of my stomach. *Not again. What did I eat this time? It couldn't be the frogs. We cooked that meat to a crisp.* No, I had never felt like this before; this was something else. *Oh my God, the mushrooms!* I crawled forward on my hands and knees, but my elbows buckled after a few feet, and I retched a volcano of vomit onto the ground, mouthfuls of liquid, gagging until there was nothing left in my stomach. Still, it wouldn't stop, and eventually something sour and burning came up, stinging my nostrils. I still couldn't see; as soon as I tried to get up the pounding came back, a vibrating chisel of pressure trying to force its way out of my temples. I collapsed back down in the dirt.

Just lie here and it'll go away. Eventually, it has to go away. Or maybe I will. I'm gone. This is it. Finally. I'm too sick to care anymore. Let it come.

Bright blue. Green. White. Orange. Eyes. A face. The eyes turned into moth wings and fluttered away. Bees buzzed in my ears, then the crunch of cracking ice echoed. Mumbled words rose and fell at different speeds, like waves in a storm. No rhythm. I couldn't understand it. *Here,* a voice said. *Drink this.*

No, I muttered. Leave me alone.

But my head was propped up anyway, something warm pressed against my lips. *You have to drink it.* It was bitter on my tongue, but I swallowed it down.

More, said the voice.

But I was already gone again.

* * *

I shivered and my teeth clicked together. I couldn't stay still—the ice-cracking noise was back. *Is that my teeth?* It was dark again. Something growled, far away in the distance, growing like a siren until it was screaming at me. Like it was right in front of my face. I screamed back.

Voices. Two soft. One hard. Or was it the other way around? *What do we do? What can we do? This is what we can do. Will she die? Don't say that! But what do we do if she does?*

Who were they talking about? Me? Just like in the hospital, talking about me like I wasn't there, like I can't hear them, like I don't have a say. The voices in my head were back again. And this time I couldn't make them shut up.

It wasn't my fault!

Oh, yes it was.

No, it was an accident.

Maybe. But it happened because of you, Emma.

It wasn't like that. It wasn't me. That old man! He had a stroke. He died. He crashed his car into us!

That's a pretty cheap shot, Emma. Blaming the dead. Remember, you weren't supposed to be driving that road.

But it was his fault!

He would have had the stroke, yes, but he would've crossed the median into an empty lane. He would have hit the guardrail, flipped his car over it, and landed upside down in the holding

STRANDED

pond. He would have been lucky—he could've gone out with a bang. But you took that away from him, didn't you? Now he's the old man who had a stroke and killed a little girl, his whole life reduced to another cautionary tale.

I'm sorry.

And you couldn't even save your sister. Really, Emma? The champion swimmer couldn't save her own sister from the backseat of an underwater car. Really?

It wasn't like that. I couldn't get the door open. It was so dark. I didn't know which way was up or down.

Excuses, excuses.

I went back, but I couldn't find the car. It was so dark.

It was only nine feet of water, Emma.

I tried. I kept going back down. Finally, I found her, I pulled her out.

But it was too late, wasn't it?

Stop it!

No.

Why won't you leave me alone?

Isn't this what you wanted? Isn't that what you've been think-ing about for over a year? For it all to be over? It can be that way, you know.

Not like this. I don't want to die like this.

Who says you get to choose?

But I don't want to now.

We don't always get what we want, do we, Emma?

* * *

Light swelled behind my eyelids, which were difficult to open, being crusted shut with sleep. Or possibly something infectious.

I pulled pieces from my eyelashes with some effort, my fingers fluttering over my face, and when I finally opened them, I saw two things: the edge of the creek bed and Oscar's back. He was dressed in his turquoise-blue T-shirt I'd seen him in the first day, but now it looked like a completely different person was wearing it.

I rolled my head to the side. I was sitting, semipropped up against a tree trunk, zipped securely in my sleeping bag, like a swaddled infant.

"Well, well, well. Look who's awake." Isaac dropped a pile of sticks next to the fire.

"How are you feeling, Emma?" Oscar must have heard Isaac, because he was now hovering over me, his eyes roving around in a long clinical stare.

"Like death."

"You sure look it," Isaac replied. "At least I thought you came pretty damn close."

My lips cracked with my smile. I still felt light-headed, but thankfully the nausea was gone. "How long was I out?"

Oscar looked away.

"How long?" I demanded, trying to sound strong, but my voice reminded me of a mouse getting stepped on.

"A day," Oscar whispered, and crouched down. "You've been out for a whole day and night."

I shrank back, but there was nowhere to go. I was horrified, and not just because he was seeing me in this condition.

Isaac shook his head slowly. "We thought you were a goner, Dodd. We all did. Well, everyone here except Wiener."

Oscar looked like he wanted to disagree. "I've never seen anyone that sick before. I had no idea what to do." He stood back up. "I guess boiling the water wasn't overkill, was it?"

The water. He thought it was the water. I didn't mention the mushrooms. How could I have been that stupid? I know how; I was starving.

"Did a plane . . . ," I began.

"No."

"Nothing?"

"No."

"They're not coming, are they?"

Oscar swallowed. "Don't know."

"It's been over a week, Wiener. You do know."

"Shut up, Isaac."

"Make me."

"I'm thirsty," I said. "And hungry."

"Good," Oscar said. "That's good. If you're hungry that means you're better."

"I had horrible dreams." I shivered, remembering.

"Fever dreams?"

"No. Not dreams even. I was just remembering."

"You screamed," he said finally. "You kept screaming the same thing over and over."

"What did I say?"

Oscar didn't answer me but shrugged as if he couldn't remember, and it was Isaac who finally told me. "Lucy," he said. "You kept screaming for Lucy."

I squeezed my eyes shut, somehow knowing he was going to say that.

"Who's Lucy?"

"It's your sister, right, Emma?" Chloe was crouched down on the far side of the fire, tossing yellow and green things into the cook pot. Dandelions. She stripped the leaves from the gold flowers. "Leave her alone, Isaac."

It wasn't a suggestion. Isaac dipped his head and pursed his lips at her.

"It's okay," I said, and pushed myself up against the tree. "Chloe's right. Lucy's my sister. Was my sister. She died last year. Drowned."

Oscar sank down, sat back on his heels. "I'm sorry." He put his head down, holding it between his hands as if it were a fragile thing that might shatter.

"I'm the one who killed her."

It was only a whisper, but loud enough for all three faces to jerk up in surprise.

I shouldn't have said that—whether or not it was true, whether or not that's what I meant to say. I shouldn't have said that. Not ever. "What I mean is, it was my fault she died."

"Can I ask what happened?"

The words came out slow, calm, the first time I explained

what had happened out loud. I sounded like I was telling a story about someone else, like I was talking about the weather. "It was a car accident." I swallowed hard. "An old man had a stroke, drove his car into ours."

"Oh." Oscar blinked. "God."

"We flipped over a guardrail and landed in a holding pond," I continued. "My little sister was in the backseat. I got out." I dropped my chin. "She didn't."

"Damn," Isaac said suddenly. "I remember that."

"What?" Oscar turned. "How do you know about it?"

"It was in the news last summer. Even made our local paper. Just a paragraph though," Isaac clarified, looking grim. "That was you?"

Just a paragraph. That's all a life comes down to, I guess.

"Yeah, it was me." I bent my head back down to my knees.

No one spoke. There was really nothing else to say.

Day 12
Late Morning

Chloe made me drink a canteen full of dandelion tea (not nearly as disgusting as it sounded) and told me what happened during the past twenty four hours when they thought I was going to kick the bucket.

It wasn't a long list.

No planes.

No food, except for blueberries.

Oscar's wrist was still injured, and everyone had decided it was, in fact, broken.

Chloe could walk. *Walk* walk. Not just gimp around with her crutch.

I hadn't noticed when she got up to fill my canteen that she wasn't using the crutch Oscar had made for her, but I watched her now. Her eyes had that gleaming look (hunger) and the same sunken sockets we all did, ringed with dark shadows, but her smile was as bright as ever.

"It's better? You can walk now?" I leaned forward, felt dizzy, then leaned back. At least I no longer smelled. Well, not like I did. Because we didn't have any more soap (only shampoo), I had used handfuls of sand to scrub the filth from my body, and it had worked surprisingly well. My sweatshirt and pants, however, were beyond saving. I left them under a sumac, the lime-green leaves already tinged at the edge with red. *The weather is changing; the trees know it. How much longer do we have before the storm arrives?*

Chloe stirred more dandelions into the pot. "You know it. Almost good as new."

"Which is why we now need to get the hell out of here," Isaac replied. "We've already wasted a day waiting."

Waiting for me. Either waiting for me to die or waiting for me to recover. I flushed in embarrassment.

"Nobody's going to rescue us. They aren't," he added quickly, as though expecting immediate disagreement, but no one argued. "Plus the storm . . ." He didn't need to elaborate. The storm could happen any day—actually, it was already a few days late. It could happen any minute. We needed to keep going. *How many more miles would it be? Ten? Fifteen?*

"I don't know if it's a good idea to move Emma yet," Oscar said, as though I were some large, difficult object. "She's barely eaten anything in two days."

"None of us have eaten in two days," Isaac pointed out, before glancing up to the sky. "We maybe have another day before that fucking blizzard drops on us."

"It might not happen. Remember?"

"Christ, Wiener! Everything that *can* happen to us has! At least everything that's super shitty. Don't you get it?" Isaac hollered. "This is no time to become an optimist!"

"I'm not," Oscar said slowly, glancing at me. "We just have to go slow is all I'm saying."

"Well," Isaac huffed. "You guys are certainly experts in that."

"Here." Chloe turned to me with cupped palms. "Eat these." She opened her hands to reveal a pile of dusty blue pebbles. "Blueberries," she said when she saw my confusion. "And I'm pretty sure they're organic."

I picked one up and turned it over in wonder, as if I'd found a diamond. A blueberry. Just like the ones my mom would buy in those plastic pints from the grocery store. We'd go through a pint in a day sometimes, and I remember tossing ones that were wrinkled or smushed on one side. It never occurred to me that there would be a day when there wouldn't be any more. There had always been more.

I put it in my mouth and pressed my tongue up, the taste of sugar immediate and euphoric. The best drug there was. I think I might have actually moaned.

"Pretty good, huh?"

Good didn't even begin to describe it. "Where did you find them?"

"When I was looking for dandelions to make tea."

"Where did you learn about that?"

"You weren't the only one reading the plant book."

"I only read about fungus." *I guess I get an F-minus for reading comprehension.*

"I found them on accident." Chloe poured the rest of the berries into my hands. "I used my shirt and made a pouch. Figured if I left I'd never find them again, so I stripped those bushes clean."

"Yeah, you should've seen it, Dodd." Isaac did his dirty-old-man grin. "Johnson here comes back just in her bra, carrying a huge sack of berries."

"Don't tell me you didn't like what you saw," she shot back.

"Okay." His grin widened. "I won't."

Oscar looked a little uncomfortable with the conversation. "We saved you an even portion."

"Thanks." I wanted to cry, but the tears wouldn't come.

"Drink more; you're really dehydrated." Chloe gave me my canteen. "Careful, it's still hot."

I took my time sipping it. Oscar got up and walked back down to the creek. Isaac went over to the shelter to gather up the supplies, and only when they were both out of hearing distance, did Chloe speak.

"What's going on?"

"Huh?" I took a gulp and singed my throat.

"Huh, what. You know what." She poured another handful of berries into my palm. "What's going on with you two?"

"Nothing."

"Riiigght." She narrowed her eyes. "So what are you waiting for? Divine intervention?"

"I don't even know what that is," I said, forcing myself to eat the berries one at a time, even though I wanted to cram the whole pile into my mouth. "And anyway, I don't think it exists." *At least not here.*

"I think you make a good couple."

"What's the point?" I wanted to laugh. "We're all going to die out here. Isaac's right. Nobody's going to rescue us."

"Maybe he is right," Chloe said, shaking her head. "But maybe we can rescue ourselves."

The cliff wasn't as high as the last one, but it was high enough, and it was steep enough that there was no easy way down. I stared for several minutes at the rock face, looking for a clue of a trail, something worn and obvious, something that showed people had gone this way before. Trampled grass, bent branches, a hole in the brush, a smooth stretch of dirt. Nothing.

"We'll have to go around," Oscar said, dejected.

"At least we have a good view up here," Chloe replied.

"Yeah, a view of trees," Isaac said. "Trees, trees, trees. Hard to tell if there's any water."

"There's lakes everywhere. We'll find something."

I put my sunglasses back on, examining the horizon. "Which way is east again?"

"There."

"I don't think we've come this way before. I would have

remembered this cliff." There was something heavy and full about the view of the woods. The silence bothered me. It was dark, even with the bright white sun beating down. The forest seemed to swallow the light; it disappeared into it like a hole, reminding me of a grave, and I didn't like the way I felt when I looked at it for too long, like I had bugs crawling underneath my shirt. "I don't want to go down there," I said, glancing at Chloe. Her face held the same creeped-out expression as mine.

"Well, that's east," Oscar repeated, as if I hadn't heard him the first time.

Isaac pointed farther down the cliff face. "It's not as steep over there. If we go that way, it will take us back down into the woods."

"Okay," Oscar said. "Let's go. I'm sure there's going to be water down there."

I scanned the tree line again, looking for an open spot, but the forest seemed to stretch unbroken in every direction. How many miles could I see? Ten? Twenty? Shouldn't we be able to see Lake Superior from here? The vastness was disconcerting, messing with my depth perception. The horizon could be ten miles away. It could be one hundred.

We went on in silence, single file, our eyes on the ground.

Unfortunately, the silence didn't last long. Curse words filled it, mainly from Isaac. I think he even started to invent new ones.

"Effendoodlebugsonofabitch!"

"You all right, Isaac?"

"Do I sound all right, Dodd?"

"You sound interesting."

Isaac snorted. "You guys are going too slow."

We were about halfway down the cliff, which was about a sixty degree angle, but much better than trying to climb down a vertical wall of rock. We were slow. Oscar was a bit ahead of us, pointing out places we should step, places we should just sit down and scoot, places we should avoid. The last thing we needed was another sprained ankle or broken wrist.

"Fine, go ahead of us," I snapped. I waved my hand at him to let him pass. As I did, I pulled out my knife from my back pocket; every time I had sat down, it poked uncomfortably against my tailbone. I moved to let Isaac get around me, and in doing so, I dropped it. It skittered down a few feet and came to rest against a rock. "Dammit."

"I'll get it." He crawled around us like a crab to get in front, retrieved it from the rock, and smiled back up at me. Or was it a sneer? "Finders keepers," he snickered.

"Give it back."

"Keep your panties on, Dodd." He flipped the blade open and examined it. "I was just kidding." Isaac started to climb back up to me, but as soon as he did, his boots slipped on some loose gravel. He dropped the tackle box to regain his balance, but his feet shot out from underneath him so quickly he had no time to catch himself. "Oh shit!"

We were still twenty yards from the bottom when he slipped, and he bounced and skittered down the entire way on his butt, gathering speed and sending down an avalanche of pebbles and dirt. He nearly clipped Oscar as he went past, cursing a streak of something completely unintelligible before he disappeared through a wall of bushes. They shook and bent and snapped and waved from the force, shivering back into place after a few seconds. There was a person-size hole in the branches, like something from a cartoon.

"Oh my God!" I said. Watching Isaac bounce and fall down the cliff like a rag doll made me feel both sick and amazed.

"Isaac!" Chloe screamed.

No answer.

Oscar was the closest. "Isaac?" He slid and scurried down the rest of the rocks, as fast as he could go safely with one bad arm, and then, after what seemed like an hour, reached the place where Isaac had gone. He looked back up at us, then ducked his head and climbed through.

"C'mon." I grabbed Chloe's arm. "Don't worry. Oscar will get him." I stepped so that I was in front, like a buffer. "I'll go slow. Just take your time, okay? If you lose your balance, sit down."

"I already am." Chloe squatted, ready to crawl down the rest of the way if she needed to.

I did the same. "Better safe than sorry."

* * *

By the time we reached the hole in the bushes, we were covered in dirt and dripping with sweat.

"Oscar?"

"Over here!"

"You okay?"

No answer. Then, "Yeah."

"Where's Isaac?"

"Over here," he repeated, somewhat softer. "Be careful coming through."

"Okay." I entered into the hole—the bushes weren't as thick as they looked, and soon enough I was down on the bottom, back in the shade of trees, though it didn't seem noticeably cooler. No breeze in here. The trees were stubby and bare, sickly looking. No birds chirping in the branches. No sound at all.

This is a bad place.

"Where are you?" Coming in from the bright sunlight made me momentarily blind.

"Over here. Be careful."

"Why?" My eyes adjusted to the dimness, and I stepped forward. A sharp crack under my boot stopped me; I looked down. Sticks. Piles and piles of dead branches, crisscrossed and covering each other, formed a very sharp carpet. It looked like a booby trap out of a bad movie, and I glanced up, half expecting a net to drop on me.

"We're over here, Emma." Oscar was off to my right, kneeling in front of Isaac.

Chloe climbed through the hole, and I held my hand up. She stopped, looked down, and nodded. We picked our way slowly over the stacks of branches. What had happened here?

"Are you okay?" I asked when we finally reached them.

"I am." Oscar stood up and moved aside, and that's when I saw that Isaac wasn't. In his tumble through the bushes with my knife, he had managed to stab himself. It was low on the left side. Two inches more and it would have missed him completely. Two inches the other way and he would have been skewered straight in his stomach.

"Oh Jesus," Chloe gasped. She covered her mouth and looked away.

Isaac smiled at us weakly. "I prefer Hey Zeus."

I took his joke to be a good sign. The blade was buried up to the handle, but there wasn't much blood around it. I hoped that was another good sign. How long had it been? Three inches? Four? It made me dizzy, imagining it. "Should we take it out?"

"No," Oscar said. "I don't know. I don't even want to try."

I recoiled. "But we can't leave it in!"

"If we pull it out . . ." Oscar shook his head, then closed his eyes and exhaled deeply through his nose. "No, it's too risky. I don't know if our first aid kits have anything to stop the bleeding."

"What about infection?" Chloe removed her hand from her mouth. "Isn't that what happens if you leave it in?"

Oscar didn't answer her, but Isaac did.

"Eventually." His eyes were like blue marbles in his face but still had that sharp, bright, bird look. "I don't know."

I crouched down. "Does it hurt?"

"No, Dodd, it tickles." He spit at me, and I noticed his spit was clean. That was good, wasn't it? No internal bleeding. "It tickles so bad I can't stand it."

"Does it hurt to breathe, I mean."

He rolled his eyes back, thinking about it, then took a short breath. "Not more than usual."

"Do you think you can walk?" Oscar wanted to know. He had taken out the first aid kit and checked what was left. Gauze pads. Tweezers. Cold pack. Splints. Band-Aids. A few packets of rubbing-alcohol pads and tubes of antibacterial cream. He took one of each.

"This ain't some boo-boo, O'Brien," Isaac said when Oscar approached him. It was the first time I had heard him say Oscar's last name. Perhaps he now had graduated up a level in Isaac's eyes. Or maybe Isaac was just terrified.

"Tell me something I don't know." Oscar eyed the handle.

"I need my knife back."

"But Emma," Oscar began.

"I know, I know," I said, and held up my hands. "I know we shouldn't. But we may need the knife. We *will* need it."

Silence.

Isaac leaned his head back against the tree. "Take it out."

"But we don't know—"

"I do, O'Brien. You need to take it out."

Oscar looked at him, uneasy, and I had the sudden idea he might want to stick the blade in farther. "I have one roll of gauze left," he said with some acid.

What I figured he was thinking: *And I really don't want to waste it on you.* I know I didn't.

Chloe pulled out a relatively clean tank top. "Here," she said. "This has some spandex in it. You can use it as a wrap over the bandage."

"If there's a lot of blood . . ." Oscar stared at the tank top, not finishing his thought.

"Wait a minute," I said, and put down my pack. "That made me remember something."

"What did? Blood?"

"Yeah." I dug down until I found my toiletry case, pulled it free, and unzipped it. "I think I put some of them in here."

"Some what?"

"Tampons." I pulled one out and held it up, still clean and sanitary in its plastic wrap. "This will work to stop up the bleeding." I pressed it into Oscar's free hand. "After all, that's what they're for."

"I have a couple," Chloe said, then looked at me curiously. "Where did you hear of that?"

"World War Two."

"Really?"

"Yeah, the medics on the battlefield used them for bullet wounds."

"Wow," Chloe said, impressed. "Who knew?"

I shrugged, secretly pleased with myself. "My dad is a big war-history buff, and I've read a few of his books."

"That's amazing." Oscar nodded and took the tampon, turning the plastic cylinder over in his hand. "But I really don't want to do this," he said quietly.

"I know. But we have to."

"If he loses too much blood . . ." Oscar's hand shook, his voice quieting to a whisper.

"I'm right here, you know," Isaac said. "I'm not deaf." Even with a stab wound, he maintained his attitude. "I'll try not to bleed on your boots."

"See?" I said. "Even Isaac agrees with me."

"I wouldn't go that far, Dodd," he barked, then winced, his face twisting back into a painful grimace. "But yeah, the knife's no good stuck in my guts."

"Okay." Oscar exhaled. "Okay, then. We'll do it." He picked up a stick and held it in front of Isaac's face. "Here, you better bite down on this." He pulled out a pack of rubbing-alcohol pads. "This is going to sting, Bergstrom." Oscar didn't sound too upset about that fact.

I crouched down in front of Isaac and eyed the handle. "I'll pull it out straight as I can," I told him. "Chloe, get the tampon ready."

"First bras, now tampons." Isaac bit down on the branch, then spit angrily between his teeth, grunting something unintelligible. Another creative obscenity, no doubt.

"Aren't you glad to have these bitches in combat now?" I whispered.

Isaac stared back at me, finally speechless.

"We'll do it on the count of three," Oscar said. "Okay, ready?"

"Wrurrdee."

"One . . ."

I pulled it out on two.

We didn't get far. A few miles. Maybe five. Probably less. We took turns carrying Isaac's things, but we left the tackle box. The fishing rod was destroyed, snapped in three places during Isaac's tumble down the cliff, and there was no way to fix it. Oscar kept the line, as well as some of the lures, a few hooks, and spinners with barbed ends. He tucked them neatly into the first aid kit. I wondered if he was planning to do surgery with them. I wondered if that was even possible.

We also didn't find any water.

"Isaac's canteen is empty," Chloe whispered to us. "So is mine. He keeps wanting water."

"I have about a quarter left," I said.

"I have half," Oscar told us.

I was surprised. Then again, I hardly saw him drink anything; he spent most of the time helping Isaac walk, but when I looked at his face, the deep rings under his eyes jumped out at me. His lips were cracked and fissured like a dried-out riverbed. "You need to drink," I told him. "Or you're going to get sick."

"I know," he said. "I just want to ration it a little longer."

"I'm going out to find water." I took my last slug, emptying my canteen.

"No, Emma, not by yourself."

"I can go faster on my own," I said. "Isaac can't, and you need to stay with them. We have no food left, and I might be able to find something."

"The sun is going to set in a few hours." Oscar's protest was a weak one. He knew as well as I did that if we didn't find water in a day or so, we'd be in even more trouble.

"That's why I'm going now," I said. "So I can be back before sunset. I'll take the whistle, my knife, and the three empty canteens. I did it before and I can do it again." I didn't know if I was trying to convince them or myself.

"Okay," he said. "But I'm coming with you. And it's not up for debate."

I stared at him; he wasn't going to budge on this, I could tell. "Okay." I sighed. "But what about Chloe and Isaac?"

"Don't worry about me," Chloe said. "I can make the shelter. Oscar's right—none of us should go off on our own."

When we headed out a few minutes later, I felt strangely energized, mainly relieved to be out of that disturbing place—this looked more like an area someone would put a campsite. And for all I knew campers could be right over the next hill.

We walked uphill, then down, before I found a small switchback trail woven between the pines. The sun moved steadily west; I knew if we were traveling east, I needed to keep the light shining behind us. I picked up a small, smooth pebble and popped it into my mouth, hoping to get some saliva flowing, and when a plane appeared overhead, so sudden and close, I almost swallowed it. Whirring propellers materialized instantly, and I wondered why I hadn't heard it coming. It streaked over the treetops, sending them waving like a wake of water. Planes only flew that low when they were looking for something. Or someone.

"Stop!" I screamed at the metal belly, but already it was shrinking away toward the western horizon. I dropped my pack and ran after it. "You're going the wrong way!" My scream was sucked up in the wind, but I kept running, remembering I had a whistle.

"Emma! Wait!" Oscar chased after me, but I didn't turn around. I just kept running, the whistle shoved between my teeth, shrieking with every step. Did it see me? No, not through these trees. But maybe it could hear the whistle. I ran like an idiot, hurdling logs, jumping and dodging, pushing through thickets, some of them probably poison oak. I didn't care. I had to make it see me. I kept running and blowing the whistle until I had to breathe, and it was a good five minutes before I realized what I'd done.

My pack. The canteens. All my supplies. Oscar. I left him. The whistle dropped out of my mouth.

No.

I shouldn't have run. I turned slowly around. I couldn't have gone *that* far.

Far enough.

I'll just go back the way I came.

Panic rose like bile in my throat. My legs trembled, but I walked, stumbling as I looked down at the ground. I looked for footprints, broken twigs, squashed leaves. It all looked the same.

The plane was heading to the lake, the lake we'd just left a few days ago.

The plane must have seen us. They must have been coming for us.

But now I would never know. I took two more steps, sank down in the dirt, and buried my face in my hands.

When I finally looked up again daylight was nearly gone, and I knew I needed to move. I needed to just go. But where? The plane wouldn't be back, at least not until morning, and I doubted it would be able to land anywhere nearby. But maybe they found our campsite, our shelter. Maybe they realized we were still alive. Maybe they were looking right now. I certainly couldn't stay here, crouched in the woods like a frightened rabbit.

I forced myself up; the whistle dangled around my neck, and I tugged the line, debating whether to blow it. What if they heard me? Start yelling? Would they even hear it? How far off was I, anyway? A mile?

"Emma!"

I spun around just as Oscar jogged into view. He was sweating heavily, somehow carrying both packs even with a broken wrist. "Emma! Thank God!"

"Oscar!" My voice broke in relief. "You're here!"

"Of course I am." He bent over, gathering a breath. "Holy crap, you run like your hair's on fire." He started laughing.

But I felt like crying. "I'm sorry!" I staggered forward and hugged him, burying my face into his neck. "I'm sorry, I'm sorry, I'm sorry."

"Hey, hey," he said, concerned. "It's okay. You're okay. I'm okay." But he hugged me back just as hard. "We'll be all right."

"No," I whimpered, now dangerously close to losing it. "The plane was on its way to that lake. I know it. If we hadn't left . . ."

The howl came as suddenly as the plane; my neck rippled with goose bumps. Then another, louder. Closer. "Oh no." I spun in circles, frantically scanning the brush. Was it in front? Behind? It seemed to be coming from all sides. *Where? Where? Where?* I had no idea. Was Isaac right? Were they tracking us? *No! Wolves don't do that? Do they?*

"We need to get out of here," Oscar said quietly, and I could hear the fear in his voice. "C'mon. Let's go." I grabbed my pack and started running, my Swiss Army knife gripped like a tiny baton in my right hand. But where could we go? Were we running away or toward them? It didn't matter; we couldn't outrun them. I heaved to a sudden halt; it was almost dark. "Wait. Stop."

"Emma!" Oscar whispered. "Don't stop!"

"We can't outrun them, Oscar."

The pines were thick and close around us. They were coming. We were the rabbits. But we couldn't hide. There was no burrow to slip into.

There was nowhere to go.

I threw my head back, a sob threatening to break from my mouth, and when I looked up, I saw the pine branches, spreading like arms above us. *Nowhere to go.*

Except up.

We left the packs at the base of the tree. I went up first, testing my weight against the branches before I grabbed Oscar's hand. Thankfully the limbs were low and thick, easy for climbing, and I pulled myself higher, five feet up, then ten, maybe twelve. I looked down; the ground looked much farther away. I swung my leg over a wide limb and inched myself forward until I was nestled in the crack where the trunk met the branch. Oscar followed until we were huddled together like a pair of baby birds.

"I hope this is high enough."

"It better be."

We stared into the twilit gloom until there was nothing left to see, and I kept my knife tight against my pounding chest, waiting.

Day 12
Night

I woke up shivering. I had no blanket, no extra clothes, not even a long-sleeved shirt.

The breeze smelled wet and cold, like snow. *The storm.* It was coming.

What time was it? I didn't remember falling asleep. But it seemed lighter; the sky was brighter through the trees. Was it the moon? I shivered again, little puffs of steam escaping my mouth as I looked around.

That's when I realized I was alone.

Oscar! Where did he go?

I needed to find him, and I needed to keep moving, if only to stay warm. I climbed down slowly, much slower than I had ascended.

I took a few unsteady steps. "Oscar? Where are you?" Already the path seemed clear under my feet, brighter where I stepped, and the sky above me wavered in a peculiar shade of green. It waved and pulsed, a giant sea with pink halos blooming and ebbing. The northern lights.

I walked on, drifting in and out of waking like a sleep-walker, talking to myself like a mental patient, when I noticed something ahead. Actually, I heard it. Music.

Old music. Big-band jazzy music, the type people danced to. Someone must be having a party. That meant people! With food! And water!

I hurried forward. *Oscar must have heard this! He must have gone this way. Why didn't he wait for me?* The trees seemed to bend away for me, ushering me past them as the light grew. Yes, I'd found a fire, probably a big campsite. I could hear laughter, voices. I was so close now. The glow rose in warm flickers between the trees.

When I came through, I finally saw them, sitting around the fire. What I had thought was a large group of campers turned out to be an old man and a young girl, roasting marshmallows—burning them to a crisp actually. The girl giggled when one melted on her stick, sacrificed to the flames. "That's all right," the old man replied with an easy smile. "We have plenty more." He looked up as I stepped into the light. "Well, hello there!"

I squinted, but it was hard to see his face in the flickering shadows. Still, there was something familiar about him.

"Have we met before?" And as I asked, I knew we had, but not in person. Not exactly. I recognized his face from the newspaper—his obituary photo.

He chuckled. "Not formally, but that's okay. You are very welcome to join us, Emma."

"How do you know my name?"

"We've been waiting for you," he said.

I stepped back, trembling. My sister Lucy pulled the blackened marshmallow off the stick with her teeth, then licked the sticky sugar around her mouth. "Have a s'more, Emma," she said. "They're really good. And I know you must be hungry."

"No!" I fell forward, screaming. "You're dead! You're both dead!"

When I hit the ground, I was still shrieking, staring up at the black limbs of the pine with wide, unblinking eyes. Oscar's silhouette peered down at me. "Emma? Oh my God!"

I had just fallen out of the tree.

"I'm okay," I choked out, and rolled over onto my stomach, gasping like a fish. Blood pooled in my mouth, and as I struggled to push myself up, I heard the snarl, so close in my ears that I jerked sideways in reflex, curling myself into a ball. Only one animal made that sound. *Wolves.* I blinked frantically, seeing nothing but blackness until the dim gray outlines took shape. The wolves stood motionless across a small clearing, camped out under another pine tree, watching me.

"I'm coming down."

"No!" *Doesn't he see the wolves?* "Stay there!"

I thought the nightmare I had had was bad. This, obviously, was worse.

"I'll climb back up," I said, still breathless, and pushed myself back against the trunk, reaching overhead for a branch. They were ten yards away, coming toward me in a steady walk. My right hand clenched the knife, but my left arm wouldn't work. It hung by my side, useless; I couldn't lift it above my shoulder to grab a branch.

At five yards the big one stopped, lowered his head at me, and curled his lips back, revealing a row of pearly teeth, the longer, crescent-shaped canines reminding me of daggers. The others stayed behind him, and I was strangely relieved to see all four. That meant they hadn't found Isaac and Chloe. Just us.

"Emma? Climb up now!"

"I can't." I flipped the blade open. It wasn't much, but right now I was grateful for something to hold on to, no matter how small.

The big wolf took another slow step, head still low, but he was no longer growling. He seemed to look through me; he cocked his head, his attention trained into the thick brush behind me. He snuffled deeply, his lips still pulled back in a hungry smile. His tongue moved across his muzzle, anticipating.

Branches rustled and snapped overhead. "I'm coming down!"

And before I could reply, Oscar was on the ground in front of me, somersaulting sideways onto his shoulder a second after landing. He swore once in pain, but popped up instantly only a few yards from the big wolf. I jumped forward, grabbed the hood of his sweatshirt and pulled him back against me, horrified and thrilled. "What are you *doing?*"

"Something really stupid," he replied weakly. "That wolf looks a lot bigger than it did from the tree."

"No kidding."

Pine bark grated against my shoulder blades. Again I reached up, but a spasm of bright pain shot through my shoulder, making me yelp and see stars. Every breath hurt; every inhalation was a stab in my lungs.

So this is it. This is how it ends. Of all the ways to go (and I had thought a lot about that in the past year), I had never imagined this. But of course it would be this way. It's always something you never expect, never plan for. *It figures.*

Halfway down, my swallow got stuck in my throat. I closed my eyes with the effort and held on to Oscar. *I hope it doesn't hurt too much. I hope it's fast.*

Something swelled behind me, rolling forward in the dark. I could feel it rise up, and even with my eyes closed my neck hairs rose. Something big. Something coming this way. My eyes snapped back open; the wolves were still crouched low, but they didn't move.

What are they waiting for?

The animal burst past us with such speed and bulk, the breeze of it tilted me sideways. As it hurtled into the circle of wolves, then cleared the waiting pack, it bellowed a moan that sent electric tremors up my legs. *A moose!* That's what they had been tracking. That's the animal that had come into our camp. And now it disappeared into the trees like a runaway bulldozer, still booming, cracking tree limbs as it ran.

The wolves turned as one, snarling in synchronicity, ready to give chase.

Day 13
Dawn

We waited at the pine tree until the sky had a lime-green edge on the horizon, and the view around us was a dim landscape of shadows. Then we started walking.

I gave the whistle two sharp tweets and waited. Silence. We walked another hundred yards, and I tried again. Nothing. On the third try I heard a tinny sound, the clang of a rock against metal.

I blew three more times. Short. Short. Long.

Three bangs echoed back, and I had to smile.

Chloe.

"C'mon." I grabbed Oscar's hand. "We're close. This way!"

Once the campsite came into view, we saw Chloe running toward us. "Did you find water?"

"No," I said, suddenly exhausted with failure. "Sorry."

She shook her head, undaunted. "I found some."

"You did?" Oscar asked. "Where?"

"It was just a dirty puddle, barely enough to swallow," she said. "But it was better than nothing."

"Oh." I exhaled, trying not to sound how I felt. "Where's Isaac?"

"There."

He was propped against the trunk of a pine tree, his sleeping bag draped around him so only his head showed. Even from this distance I saw the pale, sickly sweat shine on his face.

"He doesn't look too good," I suggested.

"He has a fever," Chloe said dully.

I glanced at Oscar; he looked wan and sick too. Fever meant infection, I knew that much.

"I heard the plane. Then I heard your whistle. I wasn't sure what to think."

"That plane buzzed over us so fast we barely saw it," Oscar said.

I nodded, dejected. "I think it was going to the lake." Had it been my idea to leave? Isaac's? I guess it didn't matter anymore. Here we were.

The sky lightened, clouded blue. Would it be sunny today? Would the watch-compass work? We should get going. We would have to figure out how to carry Isaac. We still needed to find water. We needed to keep going.

"I feel like I haven't slept all night," Chloe said. "I just need to rest." She looked over at me. Her eyes had lost their gleam. They were dull, empty. "The Zippo's done for." She held

Isaac's lighter in her hand, turning over the metal cube like a coin she was going to flip. "Then I used up the matches, but I couldn't keep the fire going with the wind. It just died."

"We should go then," I said, noticing how bloodshot her eyes were.

"Okay, but I need to rest a bit," Oscar said. "Isaac can't really walk, and he's kind of heavy to carry."

"I need to rest too." Chloe yawned and lay down, closing her eyes. "I don't think I can carry Isaac right now. I'm so tired." She rolled over onto her side.

"Okay, we'll rest a little." Their fatigue was contagious, and I sank down on the leaves.

Oscar lay down next to me. "Wake me in an hour," he mumbled into my arm.

I nodded, my head still foggy. "Okay, I will," I promised. "In an hour."

Sleep. That's a good idea. Just go to sleep.

I closed my eyes and drifted.

A buzz. A puttering hum. A mosquito in my ear? I slapped my cheek. The buzz returned.

Through slitted eyes I saw dirt. A leaf. An ant on a leaf. The sunlight slanted through the trees, late-afternoon gold. The light went away with a gust of wind, and I rolled over onto my back, forcing my eyes all the way open. The clouds were everywhere, heavy-looking. Another damp gust of wind sent shivers through my back. *Will it rain?* The clouds were definitely full; I opened my mouth when a flicker of something hit my nose. But it wasn't rain. Another splotch dissolved on my tongue. Snow.

The storm. It was here.

I pushed myself up in shock, and my head throbbed, protesting the sudden motion, but when the ache subsided, I saw everyone was in the same position.

We looked like a crime scene. We looked like dead bodies.

"Oscar? Chloe?"

No answer.

Another buzz. Not a mosquito. It was way too cold for that. What is it?

"Oscar?" It sounded like I was being strangled.

"Mmm?"

"Oscar, we need to get up. I hear something."

"Okay," he sighed, but didn't move.

I crawled over to Isaac, and his eyelids fluttered when I said his name, but they didn't open, not entirely. His shirt was darkened with sweat, and his face was bright, smoothed over with a waxy sheen like a mannequin. His chest rose and fell with the shallow speed of a bird's, heat shuddering off him in fevered bursts. "Isaac?"

"Mmm," he muttered, not really awake. "What do you want?"

"I hear something. We need to go find it."

"Go find it," he murmured blankly. Suddenly his eyes snapped open, wild and unseeing. "I would have left you!"

"Isaac, it's me . . ."

"I would have left all of you!"

He's crazy, I thought. *Or maybe he's dying. Maybe this is how it goes.* I grabbed his shoulder and squeezed. "You didn't leave us."

"Please don't!" he whimpered. "Please don't hurt me!"

"Isaac, what are you talking about?"

"Stop it, Dad! Please stop it! Don't hurt me!"

I froze. *Dear Jesus, that's who put those cigarette burns there.* "Isaac, it's all right. It's me, Emma. I'm right here. No one's going to hurt you. No one's going to leave you."

Something in my voice seemed to clear his head; the wild look in his eyes subsided. "I was going to leave!" he protested, almost crying.

"But you didn't."

"Too chicken, I guess," he sniffed, and held his hand over his eyes.

"Actually, I think it means the opposite." Even through his shirt I could feel the heat blazing off him. I remembered a picture in Dr. Nguyen's office, one of those framed inspirational prints. "If you want to go fast, go alone. If you want to go far, go together."

He choked out a weird cry. "Sounds like a bunch of hippie bullshit."

"From a poster in my shrink's office."

"Shrink, huh? You don't seem like the type."

"Eventually, I think we're all that type."

He laughed; it sounded more like a gurgle, and I saw his teeth were pink, filmed with a thin sheen of blood. I looked down and squeezed his shoulder once more. There was nothing I could do now.

"Oh God." I stood up when I heard the buzz again. "It sounds close."

"Go find it, Emma," Isaac whispered, and closed his eyes. "Just go find it."

"I will." I jerked forward, my arms out for balance, as though I was learning to walk for the first time.

Just find the noise.

I tilted forward, trying to keep my eyes open. The light was so bright it hurt. The ground moved away, and I almost fell forward. Downhill. The trail was going downhill. The noise was louder there. I shifted my weight back on my heels, letting gravity do the work.

Is this a trail? It looked like one. Wide and beaten down, dusty from use. I went faster.

Down. Down. Down.

A turn. A switchback. A huge aspen. Then blue and glittering silver, the color of water.

A lake.

Not just any lake. It was enormous. Steely blue, studded with whitecaps.

Lake Superior? I squinted, making out a dark smudge of trees on the far side. No. Not Lake Superior. But it was a lake. A large lake.

I stumbled down to the shoreline, studded with boulders the size of small cars. Gusts of cold wet air hit my face, and in my desperation to get to the water, I tripped on a slick rock and banged my knee, then my elbow. I didn't care; I was so numb I barely felt it. I stuck my head in the water, gulping at it like an animal. I didn't care about anything, only that it was wet and I could drink it.

The buzz made me lift my head and turn. About a half mile up the shoreline, on a thin crescent-moon inlet, was a dock. And next to the dock was a bright white floatplane. The buzz I'd heard was the engine; the propellers whirled until they blurred with speed.

A plane.

And it was leaving.

"No!" I waved my arms, shrieking as the pain pierced my back, but the plane taxied away from the dock, humming forward like a giant steel dragonfly, turning out a frothy wake as it gathered momentum.

"No! Wait!" I ran into the water, and when it reached my knees I fell forward. "Stop!"

I chopped through the water with sharp, quick strokes, ignoring every spasm and kicking fiercely. My clothes pulled at me. My boots dragged my feet down. I kicked harder.

I have to make them see me!

The water was icy; I gasped with each breath.

Get out there! Swim faster!

I lifted my head up to see the plane facing the opposite

direction from me. Was it going to turn? Which way would it take off?

The cold burned my hands and face, pushing me forward. Stroke. Stroke. Kick. Kick. Breathe.

Kick. Kick. Breathe.

Stroke. Stroke. Breathe.

Breathe.

Breathe.

Stop! Wait! Don't go! See me!

I looked up, but the plane wasn't turning.

No! Wait! Turn around!

Stroke. Stroke. Kick. Kick. Breathe. Choke. Cough.

The wake hit me in the face, rolling me to the side.

Stop! Come back! Please come back.

I floated on my back, watching the bright flash of white lift off, lofted up into the gathering clouds, before banking sharply over the tree line. The snow was falling faster now, like someone shaking down from a ripped pillow. The storm. Soon it might turn into a whiteout.

But I was alone, drifting along like an empty beer can.

What do I do now?

Just float. It'll be okay. Just wait a while and you'll see.

I did. After a minute the water didn't seem so cold. It felt nice. I felt nice. Numb and comfortable. My arms and legs were forgotten; I couldn't really move them much. I just floated.

Come back, Emma.

What? Who is that?

It's me, Emma. It's Lucy.

Lucy? Where are you? I don't see you.

I'm down here.

With some effort I rolled over and put my face in the water, seeing nothing but gray.

Where? It's too dark.

I know. But the dark is okay.

I tried to find you, Lucy. I did find you.

I know.

I was supposed to save you.

I know, Emma. It's okay.

It's not okay!

Oh, Emma, don't you see?

I can't see anything.

It doesn't matter. I'm okay.

It matters to me. What do I do now?

Save them.

How? I can't. It's too late.

It's easy, Emma. Just save yourself.

"Lucy!" I screamed into the water. Some primitive part of my brain forced me to breathe, and I rolled over again, back to the surface, treading water. I reached into my pocket. The knife was still there. I pulled it out, opened the blade, and held it up in front of my face, watching it flash and glint when the sun slid from behind a wall of clouds. I turned it over and over between my numb fingers. *He said it was special. He said it saved his life.* But it was just a knife, and there was nothing special about it. My numb hands fumbled; the shine from the steel glinted so bright it hurt my eyes. It spun again, once more, before it slipped from my fingers, dropping like a glimmering stone to the bottom. I drifted on. Soon enough the sun began to fade. But it was okay. I didn't mind anymore.

"Jesus, Cal, you were right! That flash? It was a person! Good Lord, Mary, Jesus, and Joseph! Hey there! Hey! Hang on! We're coming!"

Waves rose and fell, lifting and lowering me, rocking me in a frosty cradle.

"Nice and easy, now. Real slow. I'm gonna lift you up here. Good. Hang on, there you go. Cal, throw me that blanket. Holy Christ, kid, where did you come from? Can you talk? Christ, Cal, her lips are white. All right, all right. You just hang on. Cal, get on the radio to Ely. Rescue dispatch. Hang on, kid! We're going to get you outta here."

"No."

"What was that, kid? Did you say something?"

"No."

"We got to get you to a hospital, kid."

"No. Three." My teeth knocked together so hard I bit my tongue.

"Three what?"

I grabbed my own chin with my hand to get the words out. He had to understand me. I had to make myself be understood.

"There are three more."

"Three more? People?"

I made my head nod using my hand. "In the woods."

"Hey, Cal! Hang on a minute!" He took off his aviators, waved his hand, a sign to kill the motor.

"Okay, kid."

"My name is Emma Dodd."

"Okay, Emma Dodd. Can you tell me where they are?"

I forced my chin up and down, then gathered the strength to speak. "I can show you."

Beep. Beat. Inhale. Exhale.

The buzz of the machine was a low drone, much better than the high-pitched whine of insects, and I shuddered under my thermal blanket, clicking my teeth. *If I never see another mosquito, it will be too soon.*

"Wake up, Sleeping Beauty." Pause. "Or is it Snow White?"

"How about Frostbite?"

"I don't know that princess."

I rolled over. "I'm awake, but you can still kiss me if you want."

"Don't have to tell me twice." Oscar stood in the doorway, his hospital gown hanging crooked over his shoulder, revealing the deep line of his scapula. He gripped an IV pole and pushed it through the doorway. I had my own IV, attached to my wrist, giving me heated fluids, on account of what they were calling "moderate hypothermia."

"Are you supposed to be walking around?"

"Shh," he said. "Don't tell." He eased himself down on the bed next to me, and I couldn't decide if he looked like a very small child or someone who was a hundred years old.

"They're on their way?" I asked.

"Soon," he said, then nodded.

We'd only been here at the hospital for a few hours. After the pilot and copilot (both biologists with the DNR who'd been checking in on a wolf pack) pulled me out of the water, they called in the dispatch, and a helicopter had arrived. When the rescue crew saw Isaac's wound, they evacuated us directly to Duluth.

"So what's it feel like to be the hero?" Oscar studied my warming blankets, my IV drip.

"I'm not."

"You saved us all by doing what you did."

"I didn't think I was going to make it myself."

"But you did."

"Lucky for me."

"Lucky for me, too."

We sat there awhile like that, his warm hand in my cold one, listening to the machines, the movements in the building, people outside in the halls, nurses and doctors and staff, the squeak of sneakers on shiny, disinfected floors. The hum of electricity. I could turn on a light with a finger flick, turn up the heat by twirling a dial, get a drink of water by pushing a handle. The ease of meeting our needs was nothing short of staggering.

"I guess I feel even," I said finally. I didn't tell him what I'd seen in my dream, and then again what I saw in the water. Some things, I knew now, were simply beyond telling.

"Even?"

I nodded. I saved three lives to make up for the one I lost. The one I never should have lost.

Out the window was a view of the Duluth harbor, and the lift bridge was up—a huge steamer waiting for passage. Lake Superior took up the entire horizon; it became the horizon, and in this light it was impossible to tell the line of sky from the edge of water. It was everything, and soon enough the steamer would become nothing but a dark dot inside of it, chugging along on its way to the Saint Lawrence.

Oscar curled my hand up in his and squeezed it, opening his mouth to say something, when there was a commotion out in the hall. Voices rising. A nurse entered the room and, seeing us sitting together, quickly frowned.

"What is it?" Oscar asked.

"CNN, I think." The nurse blinked. "Ever since you kids arrived, all the news media in the tristate area have landed. The parking lot looks like they're waiting for the Second Coming." Her frown smoothed out; imagining this possibility seemed to please her. She looked on the far side of middle age, probably a grandmother, and she crossed her arms in satisfaction of being the first to reveal this news.

Oscar was annoyed. "They can't come in here."

"No, of course not," the nurse replied. "Over my dead body."

Interesting choice of words.

"Our parents aren't even here yet," Oscar continued.

"Some just arrived," she corrected him. "They're getting briefed by the medical team." She nodded, as if this is what she had originally come in here to tell us. "And you . . ." She crooked a finger at Oscar. "You need to get back to your room now."

"I will."

She blinked again.

"Five minutes, okay?"

The nurse made a deep *humpf* in her throat and left, still smiling.

"Have you seen them?"

Oscar nodded. "Chloe's totally fine, and Isaac . . ."

"Isaac?" I held my breath.

"I passed his room on my way here. He was eating chocolate pudding and watching cartoons."

"What? So soon? Didn't he have surgery?"

"I guess the wound missed all his vitals." Oscar shook his head, amazed. "He waved at me and offered me a spoonful. He even called me buddy."

"Wow."

"Yeah, I think they gave him a bunch of painkillers."

"That's some serious drugs."

"Yep."

More silence.

"So."

"So?"

"Now what happens?"

"I don't know." Oscar traced his fingers over mine absently. "Everything. Nothing." He shook his head. "I guess tomorrow we'll be famous."

"Don't let it go to your head."

"I'll try."

The machine beeped low. "You should probably go back to your room."

"Trying to get rid of me already?"

"Not likely."

"Good."

Voices in the hall. I recognized my mother's high-frequency pitch, my father's reassuring murmur. Other voices too. Calm and professional, trying to even out the frantic parental rhythm. They were coming, rising toward us like a tidal wave of sound.

"It's going to be weird," I said, my eyes suddenly wet.

"I know." Oscar gripped my hand tighter. "That's why I'm here. We can be weird together."

I laughed and wiped my eyes. "Then stay." Was I laughing or crying? I was happy, but tears were coming out everywhere, everything all at once, straight out of my eyes, running down my face, into my mouth, over my chin.

My face is raining, Lucy.

It's okay, Emmy, the sun will come out soon.

Oscar held both my hands in his. "You gonna be all right?"

I smiled at him, sure through my tears. Now I finally knew the answer to that question. "I am."

We squeezed our hands together and watched the door swing open.

Acknowledgments

I have been fantasizing about writing an acknowledgement page for over a decade. Because I knew even then that all things I've achieved in my life have never been done on my own. And I'm very lucky and very grateful to be surrounded by good people.

First, a huge thanks to my agent, Hannah Bowman, who not only plucked me from the slush pile, but stuck with me through countless ideas and drafts, and coached me and rallied for me and invested hours, weeks, months, and years firmly believing we would get to this point.

Secondly, to my editor Nicole Ellul at Simon Pulse, for being so incredibly enthusiastic about this story when it was only a handful of pages and a vague synopsis. Your dedication is inspiring and infectious and made this story 1000 percent better than where it started. Readers see the finished project, but they never see all the work it took to get there.

And thanks to everyone on the Simon team who put their time and effort into this book, especially Brian Luster and his insane copyediting skills. Thank you for making my writing sound coherent. Someday I may finally learn how to single space between sentences.

Thank you to my big brother, Jimmy, who took me kayaking for the first time, and told me how to make a watch into a compass. Now I know how to find my way home, as long as it's sunny out.

And most of all, thank you to my husband, Matt, and my daughter, Sena—my little north star. With you in my life I will never be lost.